WORK LIKE A CHARM

A WITCHES THREE COZY MYSTERY

CATE MARTIN

Cover design by Shezaad Sudar.

Cover images by Aarows, Yevheniia Bondarets and Stevloduv via Dreamstime.com.

Ratatoskr Press logo by Aidan Vincent Kise.

ISBN 978-1-946552-88-4

❧ Created with Vellum

CHAPTER 1

I had only been away for a week, but when Mr. Trevor turned onto Summit Avenue, I found it completely transformed from when I had seen it last. September had turned over into October, the rain had dried up, and the air had acquired a distinct chill. When I had left, the leaves had still been clinging wetly to all the trees, their green faded like the colors on a newspaper left out in the sun.

Now, everything was a riot of reds and oranges not yet succumbing to the inevitable browns. They rustled and crinkled dryly together as the chill breeze swirled through them, and their crumbling edges filled the air with that autumn smell.

Back home in cow country, we had a few trees, so I knew that smell. But here trees were all around me. That smell permeated absolutely everything.

I loved it.

"Miss Amanda," Mr. Trevor said, glancing over at me briefly as he drove down the boulevard.

"Sorry," I said, rolling the window back up. "I guess it's colder here than back in Iowa."

"Just a touch," he said, but there was a twinkle in his eye. "Happy to be back?"

"Actually, I am," I admitted. "I was only here for a few days, so I'm not sure why this feels so much like coming home. But it totally does."

"Magic," Mr. Trevor said.

"Yes, magic," I agreed, looking down at the branch that rested on my lap. I always had at least one hand on it and often found myself rubbing it between both hands during the long drive from southwestern Iowa to St. Paul. I wasn't sure if I was trying to infuse the wood with something inside myself or to draw something out of the wood into myself.

But one thing I was certain of, I had picked the right branch from the right tree for my wand. Every time I held it in my hand, it just felt so perfect.

Maybe it would help me after all. I was skeptical when Brianna and Sophie had given me a bogglingly long list of instructions for choosing and harvesting my branch. It all sounded so silly.

I mean, I knew magic existed. I had felt it flow through me. I had felt a brief moment of near-total power over everything around me.

But then it went away, and I had gone back to being my normal, powerless self. I was certain it was going to be a waste of time, going all the way back to my hometown to pick out a stick. I wouldn't even have agreed if I hadn't wanted to pack up the rest of my things, clean out my apartment, and say goodbye to the Schneidermans, who had always been like the grandparents I had never had.

Still, the moment I had stepped up to the willow tree that my father had died under, that I had been born under, where my mother had lost her voice and perhaps also a piece of her soul, I knew what I was there for was more than a simple branch.

And now I had it. I didn't know what would happen next, but I was sure Brianna and Sophie were more than ready to show me each step in a process they had gone through years before. Their own wands were a part of them now, never far from hand and always there when trouble raised its head.

I turned the willow branch over in my hands. It did feel like a part of me. I just wasn't sure it was going to be a part any better at connecting to magic than the rest of me.

"Thank you, Miss Amanda, for letting me accompany you," Mr. Trevor said as we cruised past the governor's mansion, always a hubbub of activity.

"Are you kidding?" I asked. "You were doing me a favor, saving me another two bus trips."

"Yes, but I don't get out as much as I'd like, and your hometown was full of truly lovely people," he said.

"You were quite popular, weren't you?" I teased. While I had been packing, sorting my meager belongings into what I would keep, what I would donate, and what really just had to be thrown away, Mr. Trevor had been sipping coffee at the diner counter and striking up conversations with all the locals. People who were politely friendly enough to those passing through—the diner got most of its business from travelers from the nearby highway—but were generally slow to truly warm to strangers. I don't think my mother ever was accepted as one of them, and even I was an outer tier member of the community despite being born in the diner parking lot and living my whole life in their town.

But each time I came back in to eat or drop something off with the Schneidermans or just to check on Mr. Trevor, he had a tighter group of locals around him. They traded stories and advice and recipes. When I was finally done with the final walk-through with the land-lord, I felt like I was the one pulling him away.

"You have a long list of email addresses, don't you?" I asked. "Gerta is going to send you pictures of the cookies she bakes from your old family recipe this Christmas, and Dan is going to try your technique when he fishes next weekend and is sure to send you a pic with some mammoth walleye he catches, and I'm sure tons more I missed out on."

"Email addresses, yes," Mr. Trevor said, eyes on the road. "Actually, Gerta set up a Facebook group."

"Of course she did," I said.

"You're welcome to join—"

"I'm just teasing," I said. "You made a lot of friends."

"You come from fine people," Mr. Trevor said. "But then I could have guessed that from the moment I met you."

"Oh," I said and felt my cheeks flushing. "Thanks."

"You did tell the Schneidermans they're welcome to visit any time?"

"Yes, I did," I said. "But I wouldn't get my hopes up. They would have to close the restaurant, and they still haven't even replaced me, so that's going to be tough. Definitely won't be happening this year."

"Well, perhaps you'll have to visit them instead," he said.

"Maybe," I said. "If it's possible."

My mood suddenly turned quite glum. I had a calling, a duty as a witch to guard the time portal that was anchored to the house I had inherited together with Sophie and Brianna. But that duty required a lot of magic. All three of us together, that's what Miss Zenobia had said when she had bequeathed it to us.

But I had been able to leave because, in truth, I wasn't needed. Not with my lack of ability to access magic. I couldn't even see the time portal myself. I could only access it with the pendant Miss Zenobia had crafted for her nonmagical lawyer from the past to cross over to the present on her own.

Which should have made me feel free, but I didn't. I just felt bad because I could see even in the few days we spent together before I had gone back to Iowa that our sworn duty was taking a toll on Sophie and Brianna.

They needed me to step up.

I touched the branch again, still warm from the last time I had rubbed my palms over it.

I really hoped it helped. I was prepared to work as hard as required, but I was more than a little afraid mere diligence wouldn't be enough,

"I'll drop you off at the front door," Mr. Trevor said as we neared the end of Summit Avenue. The spire from the cathedral reached higher than even the tallest trees, impressive, as the building itself was not so high up on the ridge as the palatial homes around us. "If you can get the bags in the back seat, I'll carry in the boxes from the trunk."

"I can help with that," I said.

"No, I'll have it," Mr. Trevor assured me. The house itself had no attached garage; he parked in a rented space down the hill. It was a narrow stall, one among many, the door barely wide enough for the wing-like mirrors on the sides of the old town car. I had only briefly glimpsed the interior before, as Mr. Trevor had insisted I wait in the driveway for him to back the car out. But that glimpse had been enough.

Somewhere in the home that was also Miss Zenobia's Charm School for Exceptional Young Ladies, there was a room and a little office that was his personal space. None of the three of us had seen inside it. But I was certain that the space Mr. Trevor considered truly his own was that little rented garage stall. Something about the desk with cubbies where a workbench might be more customary, the neat tools hanging from the pegboard on the back wall, the cleanly swept and oil-free concrete floor just felt like him.

Mr. Trevor pulled the car close to the curb, and I swung the heavy door open.

The rustle of the leaves. The dusty, foresty smell from above and the loamier smell from the decomposing piles below. It all swept around me like the neighborhood was rushing in to give me a hug of welcome.

I tucked the end of my branch into the back pocket of my jeans, then pulled bag after bag out of the back seat. Every bit of clothing, every boot and shoe and winter coat, I carried it all easily over one shoulder.

I remembered when I had piled it all into the car hours before, and the look that had passed over Mr. Trevor's face as he saw that the few boxes that only half-filled his trunk were all that I had in the world. He had mumbled something about a stipend and taking me shopping.

I had, after all, inherited more than a gigantic responsibility and a house that required constant maintenance to hold back the ravages of time. There was also a bit of cash. Not a lot by some measures, but more than I had ever contemplated having. That part hadn't really sunk in yet. Perhaps if it had, I wouldn't have bothered to bring back so much of my shabby, faded clothing.

I shut the door with a hip thrust, then raised a hand to let Mr. Trevor know he was good to go.

Then I just stood there a moment, breathing in that smell. It really is a fantastic smell.

The town I grew up in was dairy country. Mostly that smells like grass, which is pleasant in its own way. But sometimes it can smell a little too strongly of cow. You couldn't see cows from my apartment or from the diner, but when the wind was right, there was no way not to smell them.

I heard the sound of feet slapping on the pavement, someone jogging along the sidewalk. I opened my eyes, but the hope that had started to rush up in me quickly dampened back down. I smiled a hello at the woman who ran past me, ponytail swinging in time to her gait, and told myself I was being silly. It was two in the afternoon on a weekday. Surely Nick was still in class.

Did they call it class in a police academy? I had no idea.

The bags on my shoulder were getting heavy, the handles digging into my flesh. But I spared one last moment to look to the house next door, the one with the newly planted hostas in a row along the sidewalk.

The tall hedge blocked the yard and the lower level of the house from view. And no one was peering over it, waiting to accost me.

Not that Mrs. Olson had anything left to complain about. The first thing Sophie and Brianna had done was to fix the gaps in the magic that was letting the music from the Jazz Age bleed across time, to plague an old woman with the sounds of a never-ending party. But somehow I was pretty sure that was a temporary reprieve.

The fix would be good—Brianna was too thorough in what she did to make mistakes—but Mrs. Olson seemed the type to quickly find a new source of complaint.

And yet she wasn't around now. Perhaps it was too chilly for old bones and arthritic joints to stand in the yard and wait to spring out on passersby. Or maybe it was just time for her show. It was a couple of minutes past the hour; likely I had just missed her before she had gone inside.

But something didn't feel quite right. Not seeing her before going inside the school, it felt wrong. One thing I had been learning since coming to the school was that those feelings I had were far from delusions.

But they were also far from being clear. There was nothing more useless than a vague feeling of unease, especially when it was so dim I wasn't sure if it was really even a feeling, or at least really one of *those* feelings.

I was still standing there on the sidewalk, clutching the handles of far too many canvas bags and, I guess, consulting my feelings when the front door opened with a bang and two witches came charging down the steps straight for me.

CHAPTER 2

I admit I flinched. I mean, they had attacked me before. Granted, that had been in an attempt to trigger my magic, and they had promised not to try it again when that failed. But the sight of them charging out of the house—arms outstretched as they raced down the steps to me, Brianna's long red hair streaming in tangled locks behind her, Sophie with a crazed look in her eyes—was really rather frightening.

So I flinched and really wished the branch I suddenly had in my hand had some sort of power. But the outstretched arms closed around me in a tight group hug.

"What's all this?" I asked.

"You have no idea how good it is to see you," Brianna said, her voice muffled against my shoulder.

"Okay," I said, not sure what else to say.

"Really, it's so good to see you," Sophie added.

They were starting to freak me out a little. I had only known them for a few days, but neither of them was the hugging type.

"We just talked on the phone yesterday," I said. "You guys said things here were fine."

"We didn't want to worry you," Sophie said.

"I'm starting to get a little worried now," I said. "Can we go inside so I can set these bags down?"

"Sorry," Brianna said, and they released me from the hug. Brianna's cheeks were flaming red, although as usual, she worked not to meet my eyes. Sophie ran a hand through her short hair, leaving her bangs in a chaotic mess that she didn't even seem to notice.

Sophie never looked mussed. Now, not only was her hair standing on end, there were actual bags under her bloodshot eyes, and her complexion had an ashen hue.

I looked back to Brianna, who was gently tugging two of the bags out of my hands. I hadn't imagined it before: her usual sleek sheet of hair was tangled in matted locks, and she looked even more exhausted than Sophie.

"What's been going on?" I asked.

"Let's go inside," Sophie said, taking two more of the bags from me. "Brianna made some tea. You can have a cup while we explain."

I nodded. Just a minute before, I had wanted nothing more than a quick shower and a long nap, but now I had a lot more on my mind than the aches and pains of a long car ride.

We piled the canvas bags of my clothing at the bottom of the stairs. The doors to the parlor and the dining room stood open, but the rooms beyond were dark, the shades drawn down and the curtains closed over all the windows. That wasn't usual either.

"Did something else get loose in the house?" I asked, remembering the little demons that had attacked the two of them before. Mr. Trevor had warned me not to touch anything that looked like a container. Had something gotten knocked over and unleashed a monster?

"No," Sophie said. "We've had our hands full, but nothing has gotten away from us."

Brianna, who had reached the kitchen door, looked back at Sophie with something imploring in her eyes, and Sophie added, "we're fairly certain, anyway."

Cups and saucers were already arrayed around the table, a steaming pot waiting on the warmer in the center between a plate of cucumber sandwiches and another of shortbread cookies. I could almost feel it in the air of the room, the anxious waiting that must have been going on, the two of them jumping at every car that sounded like it was slowing down to pull up to the curb outside.

"Everything went well back home?" Sophie asked conversationally.

"Fine," I said. "It's all done. I'm here now, and I have no reason to leave again. Now, tell me what's going on."

"As it turns out, we did need you," Sophie said as she poured tea into my cup.

"For what?" I asked. "You two are the ones who can actually do magic."

"Neither of us sensed it when you were here," Brianna said, glancing at Sophie, who nodded her agreement. "Sophie noticed it first, only minutes after you were gone. It was like the fabric of the portal was… stretching."

"Stretching?" I repeated.

"Like pizza dough," Sophie said. "Have you ever stretched pizza dough?" I nodded, sipping at my tea. It was sweet and strong and just what I needed. "Okay, imagine you didn't knead the dough enough, and now you're trying to stretch it out to make a pizza. At first, it looks like it's stretching just fine, like it's supposed to. But then it gets too thin."

"It tears?" I guessed. Then nearly choked on my second sip of tea as a thought struck me. "Wait, the portal tore open?"

"No, no," Sophie said hurriedly.

"Yeah," Brianna said miserably.

"Maybe a bit," Sophie conceded. "But I felt it happening right away."

"I came up with a spell to sort of patch it," Brianna said.

"But it's like trying to patch a pizza dough by pressing down another blob of dough. It's not exactly going to work."

All of this pizza talk was making me hungry. I picked up one of the sandwiches and stuffed it in my mouth.

"You don't think anything came through?" I said, mouth still half-full.

"We watched very carefully," Brianna said. "And I crafted some detection devices. They're in the backyard now; they shriek if another tear is starting to form so we can go out and patch it when it's still just a really thin stretch and not an actual hole."

"But even with the devices, we've been watching it closely," Sophie said.

"In shifts," Brianna said. "One of us has always been awake, all week, day and night."

"And when there's a tear, we both have to be awake to fix it," Sophie added.

"I'm so sorry," I said. "That sounds exhausting." I carefully didn't mention the way the two of them were looking at the moment. No reason to rub it in. "But I don't understand what this has to do with me. Couldn't it just be a coincidence that it started right after I left? I mean, maybe it was damage from that fight. Maybe it's been slowly building since Miss Zenobia passed."

"We're pretty sure it has something to do with you," Sophie said. "Miss Zenobia said all three of us had a calling, and that guarding this portal would take all three of us together. That includes you."

"Nonmagical me," I said glumly.

"You are magical," Brianna said. "We just haven't figured out how to bring it out of you yet."

"I just really think what happened in that last fight was a onetime thing," I said. "Something was working through me. That wasn't coming from me."

"Maybe," Sophie said. I knew she could sense patterns in magic, its ebbs and flows. That fight had been too intense for her to really see what was happening magic-wise, but she must have gotten hints.

"You have a connection to the portal, I'm sure of it," Brianna said. "You did travel from 1927 back to here without a wand or anything."

"What are you talking about?" I asked.

"You followed Helen back, remember?" Brianna said. "You got back here all on your own."

"No, you brought me back," I said with a frown.

"No, I didn't," Brianna insisted. "I was working in the library when

I heard the crash of you falling in the kitchen, and Sophie and I came downstairs together and found you there with Helen."

"But you brought me back," I said again.

"No," Brianna said firmly. "I was going to, at sunset, but it wasn't time yet."

"I sent a message," I said. "I knew I had to get back early, so I sent a telegram to that other witch, asking her to contact Mr. Trevor and let him know I needed to get back straight away. So you pulled me over, didn't you?"

"I would've had to be in the yard to do that," Brianna said. "You would've seen me."

"Then how did I get home?"

"I thought that you did it," Brianna said.

"But I don't know how," I said.

"You were anxious to get back," Sophie said. "You knew we were in danger. Your urgency level must have been off the charts."

"That's a circumstance that triggers latent magic," Brianna said.

"But I didn't *do* anything," I said. "I didn't even make a wish. I was just waiting."

"And then you were here," Brianna said.

"I did see something," I said, half-closing my eyes as I summoned up the memory. "I could see, I guess, the portal itself? I hadn't seen it before."

"I really think you have a connection with it," Sophie said. "It certainly has a connection with you."

I looked down at the remains of my tea, playing over the memory and trying to remember any other little detail. But there was nothing. At the time, I had been too worried about getting home to be paying attention, I guess.

The hinges of the back door shrieked as the door swung open, and Mr. Trevor shuffled inside.

"Boxes," I said, leaping to my feet to go help him. Sophie and Brianna came behind me. Mr. Trevor had already made some trips up from the garage to judge from the stacks of boxes on the back porch.

"We can stick these in the dining room with my things for now," Brianna said, bending to pick up one of the boxes.

"Your things are here?" I asked.

"I had my roommate crate up all my stuff and ship it here. It took a week, but it turned up this morning." Despite her exhaustion, the thought of having her books back with her lit up her eyes.

"That's all of it," Mr. Trevor said, setting the stack he had staggered in with in the hall outside the kitchen. "Ah, tea. Lovely."

"We should check the time portal," Sophie said when each of us had stacked our boxes in the dining room. The few battered cardboard boxes that contained my possessions were completely dwarfed by the stacks of neatly arranged crates that held Brianna's things.

"Yes, let's," Brianna agreed.

"Me too?" I asked.

"Of course you too," Brianna said as Sophie took my hand. "We want to see how the portal responds to you being back. And who knows? Maybe you'll see it again too, like you did before."

I didn't say anything. I was pretty sure that, like being filled with ineffable power, that had been a onetime thing.

The garden had gained some yard art since I had left: a brass sundial, an ornate collection of wind-chimes that hung from what looked like an umbrella clothes drying rack, something on a pedestal that looked more like Galadriel's gazing pool than a birdbath.

Then I realized those must be Brianna's magic portal leakage detectors. They were pretty cool.

"Anything?" Brianna asked me. I shrugged. I sensed nothing more than I ever had. She blinked away a brief expression of disappointment, then pulled out her wand as she ran down the steps to join Sophie, who was already beginning her spinning, arm-sweeping dance among the plants.

I watched the two of them for a while. Then I tried half closing my eyes, trying to settle into a more meditative state. Then I tried just staring really hard until I saw spots dancing across the sky. But that was nothing more than the usual side effect of staring into the bright sky for too long.

Then Sophie ended her dance, holding the last pose for a long moment before letting all the tension drain from her body as she turned and walked back to the porch where I sat on the steps.

"Anything?" she asked me.

I shook my head. "What did you sense?" I asked.

"It's back to how it was before you left," she said. "We're going to want to keep an eye on it for the next few days to be sure, but it's definitely better with you here."

"I wish I could watch it for you and let you both get some rest," I said.

"No worries," Sophie said. "We'll have you working beside us soon enough."

"Sophie and I have your training regime all planned out," Brianna said, and her eyes lit up again. "We wanted to get started straight away. Dawn tomorrow."

"So you're the one who should rest up," Sophie said. "We're going to be very demanding teachers."

"I'll be the best student," I promised, although to be honest, I had only been an average student back in my school days. Still, I had no need to learn any of that stuff. This was very different.

I went upstairs to finally get that shower and nap. It was only as I stood under the deliciously hot water that I remembered about Mrs. Olson. I had meant to ask Sophie and Brianna if they had seen her lately, but after everything they had told me, I wouldn't be surprised if they had been too preoccupied to notice if and when Mrs. Olson had been out in her yard.

I told myself it was nothing. A woman her age couldn't just stand around the yard all day.

But that feeling in my gut just wouldn't go away. Something was making me feel uneasy. Was I sensing the weakening of the time portal, only now beginning to recover from my absence? Maybe I was sensing magical things and just didn't know how to assign meanings to these vague feelings.

Perhaps things would be clearer in the morning when my training started.

CHAPTER 3

*I*n through the nose, out through the mouth. In through the nose, out through the mouth.

The coldness of the wet ground under my yoga mat was starting to seep through. I could feel the backs of my thighs losing warmth, like it was being drained off by a vampire. Maybe I should have moved around more before I came outside with Sophie, gotten more of the kinks out before sitting down. But then it still wasn't even dawn yet. I was an early riser, but there were limits.

I sighed. I was thinking thoughts. I wasn't supposed to be thinking thoughts. I focused on my breath again.

In and out. In and out.

I could just hear the stirrings of Sophie's own breath as she sat in front of me, close enough to touch if I reached out a hand. Her breathing was slower even than a sleeping person's, and she wasn't fidgeting at all. Was her mat thicker? My legs were going numb from the cold and from being folded up too long. I twitched a toe, making sure I could still feel it. It certainly felt cold enough for frostbite, October or not.

I was thinking thoughts again. Ugh. I was never going to master this not thinking thing.

Slow breath in through my nose. Hold it for a moment, then slow exhale through my mouth. This time, I managed to just breathe for what felt like several minutes.

Did I sense anything around me? I felt a little dizzy, but that was it. Then I was all too aware of the cold again and longed to clap my hands together and stomp my feet.

"And done," Sophie said in her softest voice. I opened my eyes. She smiled over at me. "How was it?"

"I don't think I was doing it," I admitted. "I'm cold."

"Oh," Sophie said, and I swear I could see the instant she became aware that it was cold. How had she tuned it out? "We can do this inside next time. But I wanted you close to the time portal the first time to see if you sensed anything about it?"

I shook my head. "Did you?"

"Yes," Sophie said, looking up at the tops of the trees in the orchard. "Whether you know it or not, it's doing much better with you here."

"That's something, I guess," I said, stretching out my cramped legs.

"Let's try a moving meditation," Sophie said, rising up to her feet with the grace only a lifelong student of the ballet could make look so effortless. She lifted her arms and started to dance in slow circles.

"What do I do?" I asked.

"Whatever feels natural," Sophie said, her eyes closed as she spun around me. "Just… lose yourself in the movement. Feel how your muscles move, but don't try to control it. Just let go."

I could already tell this wasn't going to go well. I half-closed my eyes and decided against spinning, as my head still felt a little swimmy from the breathing before.

I opted for a sort of skating motion, long, slow strides from side to side with arm swings to match. I had never taken to figure skating, but years of hockey made the motion second nature to me.

I think I almost did get lost in the motion, for a split second anyway.

Then I tripped over the edge of a raised garden bed.

I stumbled, eyes flying open, and recovered my balance without falling to the ground. But I only made a few steps further before my foot slid over the dew-wet lawn. I opted to fall backwards onto my butt to avoid slipping into an involuntary splits. Flexibility had never been my strong point.

Sophie continued spinning around the orchard, oblivious to my difficulties. I tried to get back into motion, but now I was super paranoid about hurting myself and got nowhere near the mindless state I was supposed to be reaching for.

Finally, Sophie came to a stop, stretching her upper body down towards the ground, then straightening up slowly, one vertebra at a time.

She was smiling at me again. "How was that?" she asked.

"Yeah, not good," I said, brushing grass and dirt from the seat of my pants.

"Well, don't be too down," Sophie said. "It's just the first day."

I nodded, but I saw the disappointment in her eyes. She had hoped for something a bit more hopeful from me.

I went into the kitchen and poured myself a cup of coffee, then added a spoonful of butter, stirring until it melted and gave the surface of the coffee a slick sheen. I took a little sip, then a bigger gulp, before heading out into the hallway.

I had come down the back stairs after Sophie had woken me, so I hadn't noticed that the dining room looked like a small tornado had blown through it. Every crate was at least half open, some of the contents pulled out and stacked on the massive table in haphazard piles.

I was pretty sure the small tornado had been named Brianna. I shivered to think what she had in store for me, but at least I would have some coffee in me first. I took another long swallow, then headed up the stairs to the library.

The library was dead quiet, the kind of quiet you only get when row after row of tomes was absorbing every decibel of random noise. Even the sounds of morning traffic that had been perfectly clear as I climbed the stairs faded completely the moment I had books on all sides of me.

Brianna was at the largest table in the center of the room, one finger marking a place in a book the size of an atlas as she wrote something down with her other hand. The scritch of her pen across the page was a comforting sound.

I waited for her to finish the sentence and look up at me, but her writing went on and on, her eyes moving from the finger on the book to her own scribbling and then back again. It was only when she turned the page and started writing again on the top of the new page that I realized she was completely unaware of my presence.

For some reason, I thought of the conventional wisdom not to wake a sleepwalker. It felt like it also applied here.

I cleared my throat. Then I stepped closer, bending low so that my face was in her field of view. But still, she didn't notice me.

"Brianna?" I said as softly as I could.

Brianna kept on writing. If anything, the expression on her face grew a bit tighter, like she was actively tuning me out. Not intentionally, just as if a part of her was aware there was a potential distraction and redoubled her focus without exploring what the distraction might be.

"Brianna," I said again, more loudly. She blinked and looked over at my coffee mug sitting beside her cooling cup of tea.

"Oh, Amanda," she said. "Good, you're here. How did it go with Sophie?"

I started to try to mumble a reply, but to my relief, she didn't wait for an answer, just brushed past me, catching at my elbow to direct me to follow her. I picked up my coffee and carried it past three more rows of bookshelves to a smaller table at the back of the library. I remembered it well; I had hidden beneath it the day the two of them had tried to trigger my latent magic by attacking me. Was that why she had chosen it?

"I think you'll find it quieter here, away from me," Brianna said. "I don't want to distract you while you study."

I strongly suspected she really meant the reverse, but summoned up a smile of thanks, anyway.

"I've chosen the most basic of my magic texts for you to start with," Brianna said, and I nearly choked at the sight of the massive tome waiting for me on that table. It lay open, a small weight shaped like a curled up cat holding the front cover down. The writing was so tiny, and it filled the page with no drawings, no charts, and only the narrowest of margins at the frayed edges of the page.

This was the most basic book she had?

"And this is a gift," Brianna said, thrusting a smaller book into my hands. I quickly set my coffee aside to take it. The book was smaller than the tome, small enough to fit inside a purse, but thick. Like a leather-bound brick of paper. The leather and the paper both smelled new, and when I opened it up, I found all the pages were blank. "It's a journal. You can use it to organize your own thoughts about what you are reading. It's the best way to learn, like interacting with the text. I have tons."

She looked insanely pleased. I mustered up a smile. "Thanks. This is great. So, what do I do?"

Brianna's happy smile faltered a little. "What do you mean?"

"Do I have an assignment or something? Like in school?"

"No," Brianna said. "It's more a self-directed study."

"I don't think I got as much out of my school days as you did," I said.

"This isn't like school," Brianna said. "It's more interesting because it's stuff you can use."

"Maybe," I said, touching the completely intimidating tome waiting for me on the table. "What if I don't understand something? Do you want me to ask you?"

Brianna chewed her lip and frowned. I think we were both picturing the same thing: me interrupting her work every minute or two to ask another question, the answer to which would probably seem completely obvious to Brianna.

"You can make a list," she said at last. "We'll go over it together at lunchtime. Then I can show you the main source books and how to use them. I'm sure you'll be finding your own answers in no time."

I was somewhat less sure, but I still gave her a reassuring smile and shooed her back to her own table. Whatever she was working on probably was really important. I shouldn't be a distraction.

I sat down at the table and set my journal down on the table, standing on its spine. I opened both covers and flattened them down, then paged both sides closer to the center and flattened them down again, then again and again until I was in the center of the book.

The thing is, I did love books. I didn't own many, but I had been a constant presence in my local library. But my preference had always been for fiction. I had consumed stories like a fiend.

I set the journal down flat and took up the pen Brianna had left for me, then looked down at the first page of the tome. I doubted very much this was a story that was going to sweep me up and carry me away to a land where time flew by as I turned the pages.

But still, I was in a warm, cozy library with a hot mug of coffee, and my only job was to read and make some notes. After so many years working long shifts on my feet all day in a chronically under-staffed diner, this was practically a vacation.

I mean, how dry could a book be?

CHAPTER 4

Time did not fly. I never even got to turn a page. I did compile a truly impressive list of questions, and the growing sense I should probably set this book aside and devote myself to learning Latin first, and probably also Greek.

When Mr. Trevor stepped up behind me to ask me if I was hungry for lunch, I had never been so happy to see anyone in my life.

Sophie and Brianna were both already in the kitchen, Brianna with a book open in front of her as she sipped at a mug of tomato soup and munched on a cheese sandwich.

"How was studying?" Sophie asked as I set my journal down and helped myself to one of the pile of sandwiches.

"I'm not sure that's what I would call what I was doing," I admitted.

"You have questions?" Brianna asked, shutting her own book a bit wistfully and directing her attention towards me.

"So many questions," I said, sliding my journal over to her. Mr. Trevor brought me a mug of tomato soup, and I smiled my thanks at him, then took another bite of the sandwich. Sophie watched as Brianna scanned down the list of my questions, then turned the page to continue scanning, then turned yet another page. Her eyebrows lifted higher as Brianna turned page after page.

"That bad?" she asked.

I shrugged. "It's a bit over my head. Have you read it?"

Brianna looked up at us. "I tried to get her to before, but she was busy."

"So busy," Sophie said, dunking her sandwich in her soup.

"Doing what?" I asked suspiciously.

"Not reading that book," she admitted with a grin.

"It's such a good book, though," Brianna said, genuinely distraught. "I learned so much from that book. It was a jumping off point to so many other lines of thought."

"Like string theory and magic branes?" I guessed.

"No, that came much, much later," Brianna said, staring glumly down at the crusts of sandwich left on her plate.

"How old were you when you read that book?" I asked.

"The first time? Six," Brianna said. "It changed my life."

"I think the life-changing book I read at six was probably something by Dr. Seuss," I said, and Sophie had to smother a laugh as Brianna looked up at us with something like hurt in her eyes.

"*You* should write something," Sophie said to her. "I'm sure you could convey the basic concepts in a much more relevant way to modern audiences."

"That would take so much time, though," Brianna said. "I already have so much to do."

"Look, I'm not ready to give up yet," I said, giving her hand a squeeze. "I don't think I'm ready for that book yet either; it assumes a lot of knowledge I don't have. I might have to bone up on other stuff first. Like Latin, for instance."

"Miss Zenobia has tons of Latin textbooks in the library," Sophie said. "I think she probably taught it to her students."

"And if that doesn't help, I can head out to the closest public library and see what they have," I said. "I need to get a card, anyway."

"All right," Brianna agreed. "But not just now."

"I don't think I'll get much value out of spending more time on that book," I said.

"No, studying time is done for the day," Sophie said. "We're taking you downstairs."

"Downstairs?" I said. The building had a cellar, but it wasn't accessible from inside. We had to go out to the yard and pull open the heavy storm doors.

It was like walking down into a cave. A really cold, really dark cave.

I couldn't see a thing, so I guessed there were no windows. I could smell wood smoke, kind of ashy, like it had burned down, but the embers were still hot. But there were other smells, too. A pungent odor like bad incense, a sickly sweet odor like someone had spilled soda syrup under a machine where no one could reach it to clean it up, and it was slowly evaporating into the air. There were some chemical smells as well, solvents or preservatives or something.

Under all of that, I could just get a whiff of the smell I had actually been expecting: the musty cellar smell of home canning jars left too long on a forgotten shelf and the mummified remains of long-dead rodents in the darkest corners or maybe in the walls themselves.

Then I heard Brianna murmur a word and suddenly there was a warm fire glowing in the belly of an old-fashioned iron stove. The door stood open, letting as much light as possible permeate the room, but Brianna was rapidly adding to that, touching candle after candle with the tip of her wand until the entire space was filled with golden light.

"What is this place?" I asked as my gaze swept around the room. It was about half the size of the building above us, all one grand room but with different areas set off from each other, like learning stations at a science museum. One corner was filled with candles hanging in pairs from drying racks by their long, conjoined wicks. Halfway down the room was a series of tables arranged close to a fireplace, the tables covered with tubes and flasks and great bubbles of glass, like something out of an alchemy textbook. Another looked like a kids' crafting station, with little drawers overflowing with buttons and feathers and shells.

"Every witch needs a laboratory," Brianna said. "There are all sorts of magic, after all. Potions. Amulets. Dolls. Herbs and medicines. Baked goods."

"Baked goods?" I said. "Wouldn't the kitchen upstairs be better for that?"

"Sometimes the old ways are best," Brianna said, running a hand over the metal door of the oven built into the fireplace. "The sort of wood you burn to heat the oven is part of it. Can't do that upstairs."

"I suppose not," I said. "And you two know how to use all of this stuff?"

"Not yet," Brianna said. "Once I get a handle on what I'm working on upstairs in the library, I plan to start a series of experiments—"

"But that's not why we're down here today," Sophie interrupted what we both knew was likely to be far more detail than we wanted to know about Brianna's plans. Because the details would be so far above our heads, it would all be meaningless to us. "It's time for you to get to work on your wand."

"Oh. Good," I said, trying not to sound as nervous as I felt. "But should this really be the first thing I do? Shouldn't I learn the basics first?"

"You'll learn by doing," Brianna said. "It's fine. It's witch tradition. You're no further behind than the other kids."

"Kids," I said, remembering that the two of them had made their wands when they were quite young.

"Here," Sophie said, holding out a cloth-wrapped bundle to me. I took it from her and unwrapped what looked like cheesecloth to expose the stick I had brought back from Iowa. "Brianna and I can't touch it."

"Why?" I asked.

"Everyone's magic is different," Brianna said. "It pulls from different sources; it channels differently through your body."

"Touching another witch's wand is like someone using the spoon for the blue cheese dressing to serve themselves some balsamic vinaigrette at a salad bar," Sophie said.

"Gross," I said.

"Yeah," Sophie said. "You just corrupted a spoon and two dressing containers."

"It's not so bad as all that," Brianna said. "It is best to never touch another witch's wand, but in dire circumstances, a little common sense is required. It will affect your spell, and you can compensate for that if you know the witch and have a sense of their magic, but it will only affect the wand if it's done repeatedly, or if it a particularly powerful spell."

"No worries there," I said under my breath.

"But before the wand has been fashioned to meet your specific magical energies, it is absolutely crucial that no one else handle it. I know we didn't explain why before you left, but I hope you followed the rule in that?" Brianna asked.

"Of course," I said, turning the stick over in my hands. "I took it from a higher branch in the tree, and no one since has touched it but me. I'm absolutely sure of that."

"Very good," Brianna said with a nod. Then she led me to the furthest corner, where a pegboard on the wall held an array of woodworking tools. A bench stood beside it with a vise attached to one end. Everything was covered in sawdust, but it didn't smell fresh. I suppose it had been decades since Miss Zenobia had brought a class down here.

"What do I do first?" I asked.

"There's a lot of spellwork involved later, but for now you just need to shape it," Sophie said.

"Peel off the bark, whittle it down to the size that feels right to you, and sand it all smooth," Brianna said.

"Take your time with it," Sophie said. "It will become a part of you, probably for the rest of your life. Don't rush any of the steps."

"Got it," I said, turning the branch over in my hands. "This I can do. I had lots of shop classes in high school, and woodworking was always my favorite."

Brianna gave me a relieved smile, but then her face turned grave again. "Except for the steps where it has to dry overnight, keep it with you even when you're not working on it. Never leave it in your room again."

"We should have told you that before," Sophie said. "Although it took me a bit of hunting to find it, so I know you were being careful. But it should really never be out of your possession."

"Why?" I asked. "If I never master any magic, it's going to be kind of worthless."

"Don't say that," Sophie. "We're going to find your magic."

"It's important that you never lose it, and absolutely crucial that it never gets stolen," Brianna said. "A destroyed wand can be replaced, but the replacement will never be the same. A witch's bond with her wand strengthens over time. With a new wand, you have to start over, and you'll never get back what you had."

"Okay, that makes sense," I said, looking down at the branch I was about to connect my soul with.

"There's more," Brianna said. "A destroyed wand can be replaced, but a lost or stolen one cannot. If your wand still exists anywhere in this world or any other, no other wand will bond with you. You will be wandless."

"Some magic is possible without a wand," Sophie said, and I knew that was true. I had seen her do many things using her dancing as the conduit.

"But it's less powerful magic," Brianna said. Sophie looked like she wanted to argue, but Brianna quelled her with a look. "I know you prefer to work without it, but it's always with you. It supports you, whether you know it or not."

"You make it sound like a living thing," I said.

"When you're done with it, it will be," Brianna said.

Then the two of them left me alone to select a knife and get to work on scraping off the bark and knots from the wood.

I didn't know what was going to come next, but this part felt downright comforting in its familiarity. I even started to whistle as I worked.

I could do this.

CHAPTER 5

"*I* can't do this," I said, head in my hands as I ignored the food in front of me.

"You're just getting overwhelmed," Sophie said, giving my arm a squeeze.

"Yes," I agreed. "That's it exactly. Overwhelmed. Not sure where the 'just' comes in, though."

"You can't give up," Brianna said.

"It's been days," I said. "Days and days of failing to meditate properly, failing to sense the magic around me even when I'm apparently standing in the most active part of the time portal nexus. Failing to grasp even the most rudimentary parts of magic because I don't even understand the words."

"It will get easier," Brianna said.

"It's barely been a week," Sophie said. "Maybe we're working you too hard. Maybe you need a break."

But Brianna had been speaking at the same time, and although she had spoken in that soft voice she used when she was mostly thinking out loud, I hadn't missed what she was saying. She thought I should work harder. She thought more hours of study per day were called for.

Sophie must have heard her too, to judge by the glare she shot her.

I put my head back down into my hands.

"Hey, look on the bright side," Sophie said. "Your wand should be ready today."

"Yes, the last coating of oil is sure to be dry by now," Brianna agreed. "Eat something, and we'll go down and check it out."

It's not like the food didn't look good. Mr. Trevor always seemed to know just what I was craving. And even though I was cranky and overwhelmed and frankly exhausted, it was turkey and Swiss on fresh-baked croissants. It wasn't a hard sell. I ate one in two monster bites, then took another one with me as we went out to the backyard, then down to the cellar.

I wasn't much of a fan of dark, damp spaces like windowless cellars, and no matter how hot we ran the iron stove, the cold seeping in through the stone walls was bone-chilling. But sitting close to that stove, whittling and sanding, then oiling and polishing my wand, had gained a certain comfortable familiarness. Brianna seldom strayed out of the library for more than a quick look at my work, but Sophie tended to linger in one of the other corners of the cellar. She didn't seem to be working on any particular project, just going through all the drawers and nooks and boxes up on shelves. There was more than enough to keep her busy until spring just looking at it all, I was sure.

I had left the wand standing upright in the vise while the last coat of oil dried. It wasn't a wood preserving thing; it had been some sort of magical ointment that Brianna had shown me how to cook up using that scary alchemy equipment. It gave the branch a smell, sort of like sandalwood but with a hint of something almost minty.

The stain I had rubbed into the wood had turned the willow a rich, dark reddish-brown that gave flashes of a more golden hue when it caught the light just right.

I admit, I thought it was all kinds of beautiful. If it were possible to crush on a stick, I would say that was pretty close to what I was feeling.

But it was supposed to feel like an extension of myself, not just a pointy projection from my hand but a part of my very soul. As much as I loved it, and I did love it, it was still very much a thing I just longed to bond with.

"You've done very nice work," Sophie said.

"I made a pretty stick," I said. "It remains to be seen whether it's anything more than that."

"Try it out," Brianna said.

"What do you mean?" I asked.

"Just swish it around a bit, see what happens," she said.

I felt extremely self-conscious, the two of them watching me intently while I raised the stick high like a conductor's baton, then gave it a little stir.

Nothing.

They were looking at me eagerly, like they were still waiting for sparks to fly. I shook my head.

"Try really focusing," Sophie said. "Think of yourself flowing through the wood. It concentrates power that otherwise sort of floats in a cloud around you and through you. Think of it like that, like a prism making a laser light or something."

"Try it," Brianna said.

I closed my eyes and tried to imagine a feeling like what Sophie was describing. Then I waved the wand again.

Nothing.

"What's supposed to be happening here?" I asked with a sigh. "Sparks or a rainbow or what?"

"Could be anything," Brianna said.

"Did you feel anything trying to happen?" Sophie asked.

"No," I said, and bit down on my lip.

"Well, that's okay," she said. "I took a long time to bond with my own wand. It doesn't have to happen right away."

"It's really okay—" Brianna said, but I just couldn't take it anymore.

"I'm going for a walk," I said.

"Amanda," Sophie said.

"I'm fine," I said, although I was far from it. I was really afraid I was going to start crying there in the cellar, and the last thing I wanted to do was break down. Sophie and Brianna were already upset enough as it was. I knew they were blaming themselves for being inadequate teachers, even though it was clear I was just a lousy magical student.

The idea of crying in front of them was just too much. "I've got to go," I said, and pulled my hoodie more tightly around myself as I headed for the stairs.

Brianna started to call my name, but Sophie caught her arm and held her back, whispering, "let her go."

The overcast day matched my mood perfectly. Gray clouds hung low in the sky in swooping patterns like furrowed eyebrows, an occasional blacker cloud speeding under that oppressive canopy as if even it wanted to escape it all.

I was a couple of blocks away before I realized I was still clutching my wand. Out in public. I tucked it in my back pocket, pulling the back of my hoodie over it, then thrust my cold hands deep into my pockets.

Brianna had been studying magic in the company of actual witches her entire life. Even Sophie, who had lost the only witch she knew when her mother disappeared a decade ago, had gotten a head start on me when she started learning simple magic as a little girl. But if my mother had remembered any of the magic she had known, she had chosen not to teach any of it to me. And now I really needed it. Sophie and Brianna were counting on me. Was I too old to learn this stuff now?

I had been a conduit to a power that wasn't mine. And at the time, it had seemed like I was the one making the choices about what I was doing with that power. But had I really? Or had I just been doing what some other more powerful being wanted?

Helen had been messing with things she ought not to have been messing with. She had angered something; I had felt that.

But no, in the end, I had chosen to spare her. That had been my choice; I was absolutely certain of that. I had chosen mercy. I had chosen to turn Helen over to the authorities in 1927 and not to just end her life, even though she had tried to kill the three of us and had succeeded in murdering her own sister and her sister's husband.

I touched the pendant I always wore under my clothes. Cynthia's pendant, very briefly Helen's, now mine.

I might never wield power of my own, but I still made my own choices.

I sighed and turned to walk back to the school. Clearly, all the early mornings were wearing on me. Too much trying to focus, too much inner reflection, definitely too much time trying to make sense of dense old books. I needed a break, and I was going to have to demand one, whatever Sophie and Brianna said.

If I could just stop trying to do the impossible for a day or two, perhaps I could tackle it fresh, maybe change the results. I wouldn't know until I tried it.

I knew that continuing to grind away wasn't doing me any good.

I heard footsteps slapping on the sidewalk, coming towards me, and lifted my head, pushing my hood back as I saw Nick heading my way. I only really grasped how angsty I had been being in that instant when those green eyes met mine, and my mood changed like he had somehow flipped a switch in my mind.

Wow, had I been wallowing fruitlessly in negativity.

"Nick!" I said. "So good to see you! I've been back for days but so busy all the time. I guess you're probably busy, too. How's police academy going?"

On some level, I knew I was talking way too fast. At least I didn't blurt out loud that I had been looking out the windows every spare moment I could find, hoping to see him jogging by with his grandfather's Irish setter, Finnegan, keeping pace beside him.

"Fine," Nick said, but he wasn't. The worried lines on his forehead were working overtime, deep and furrowed, and I felt bad for not noticing it when he had walked up to me.

"What is it?" I asked. "Oh no, not your grandfather?"

"No, no, he's fine," Nick said. "It's Mrs. Olson. Have you seen her lately?"

"As a matter of fact, I haven't," I said, and felt a rush of guilt. I had been so consumed with my attempts at activating my magic, I had completely forgotten my own worry about Mrs. Olson. "I wasn't sure if that was odd since it's so much colder now than it was before I left."

"I don't know," Nick admitted. "Usually I only stay with my grandfather in the summertime. This is my first autumn here. But I'm so used to seeing her. I feel like something might be wrong."

"I feel it too," I admitted. "Does she have anyone to check in on her? Family or someone who comes in to tidy up or something?"

"I'm not sure," Nick said. "Her husband and only child both passed, but maybe there's a cousin or something. I don't know. Maybe I'm panicking over nothing." He sighed and ran a hand through his hair, long enough to spill over his forehead now. "No, I don't think it's nothing. Is it nothing? I'm used to trusting my gut."

He was looking at me like I could somehow tell him whether he was being irrational or not.

Maybe I could.

"You know what?" I said, catching his arm to lead him back down the sidewalk. "This is silly, both of us worrying about this. Let's just go up to her house and knock on her door. We'll both feel better when she answers, even if she takes us to task for interrupting her stories."

"I knocked before," Nick said, but let me pull him along. "But that was a couple of days ago."

"Let's check again, and if she doesn't answer, we can plan the next steps from there," I said.

"Like what?" he asked, glancing sideways at me. As usual, those eyes made little shivers run up and down my spine. Rather like I expected, my own magic would feel if I ever tapped into that.

"Oh, the usual," I said. "Peeking in the windows, pawing through her trash. But we'll start with knocking on the door."

Nick laughed, and somehow that sound just evaporated the last dregs bit of my dark mood and lifted the cloud of exhaustion off my brain.

If only there were some way to get Nick to pitch in with the whole magic thing. I just knew with him there cheering me on, I could do anything.

Alas, the whole being a witch with no magical powers thing was hard to explain. He would just think I was crazy.

But at least in the meantime, we could solve a little mystery together. A little missing persons case to put on his resume, and him not even out of police academy yet.

But I was probably getting ahead of myself. How much could really follow a simple knock on a door?

CHAPTER 6

$\mathcal{I}$ glanced over at Nick walking beside me with his hands buried deep inside his jacket pockets. He looked even more down than I had been feeling before he had shown up.

Maybe I could cheer him up?

And, you know, not dwell on the fact that seeing me hadn't filled him with joy in the same way I had been filled seeing him.

"Thanks for doing this," he said before I could come up with anything to say. "I know I could just go up and knock on her door again myself, but I'd rather have some company. I'm glad you're back."

"I've been back for about a week," I said. "I guess we've been missing each other."

"Yeah," he said, sounding distracted.

"Police academy must keep you busy," I said, but he just shrugged. I was starting to feel like I was needling him for information. "So I guess this is where I live now," I said instead. "It's a big change for me."

"It's a cool place," Nick said, making some effort to hold up his end of the conversation. "Lots of history."

I almost laughed out loud. How little he knew how close that history was.

"I lived my whole life in that town. The place where I was born, the apartment I lived in, the schools I attended and the diner I worked in were all within walking distance of each other. Now, I don't even know where the closest library is."

Nick looked up as if he could spot such a building. Then he took his phone out of his back pocket and poked at the screen as we walked. "Take a right on Kellogg and walk down towards the river. It's about twenty minutes away."

I grabbed his wrist a bit too eagerly to see the map on the screen. I had a smartphone, but the maps app frequently had a hard time figuring out where I was and what direction I was facing. Like I needed any help in getting lost.

"Thanks," I said.

He was grinning at me as he put his phone away. "Clearly libraries are important to you."

"We actually have one in the school, but hardly any fiction," I said. "I'm jonesing."

"The school?" he said.

"The house," I said. "It used to be a school. There's still a little plaque by the front door. MISS ZENOBIA WEEKES' CHARM SCHOOL FOR EXCEPTIONAL YOUNG LADIES."

"So you have a library full of books to learn how to be charming?"

"Something like that," I said, feeling my cheeks turning pink. Perhaps he'd write it off as from the chill in the wind.

"Well, don't overdo it," he said, glancing over at me again. "You already have more than your fair share. No need to rub it in."

"That's just small town politeness," I said, my cheeks heating even more.

"I've been to lots of small towns," Nick said. "Politeness is just charm on the lowest setting."

He was looking at me again, and I was getting flustered. So flustered, in fact, that my hand was starting to reach for the wand tucked in my back pocket to have something to fidget with. I caught myself just in time, shoving my hands into my front pockets to keep them out of trouble.

A sudden memory washed over me, dinner with the Schneidermans in their home with Mr. Trevor. Mrs. Schneiderman was the closest thing I'd ever had to a grandmother, so perhaps it hadn't been so odd when she asked me if I had met any nice young men in St. Paul. I had stammered some reply about only having been in the city for a few days and being very busy, which prompted more waffling and spinning as I had begged Mr. Trevor not to tell them that there had been a murder on the property and I certainly couldn't tell them about the magic. Which led Mrs. Schneiderman to conclude that I was pretending to have been busy, but had in fact been deeply smitten with someone. So much teasing for the rest of dinner—heck, for the rest of the week—and the constant paranoia that Mr. Trevor would let something slip.

Not that Mr. Trevor had any reason to know what I was feeling. Surely I wasn't such an open book.

Was I?

"So, you were moving as well?" I said, perhaps a bit too forcefully.

"Yes, into my grandfather's spare room. Which is really his office, but he doesn't work anymore, and it has a pullout couch," he said.

"I hope it's a nice one," I said.

"Not really," he said. "There's a bar that runs right under my shoulder blades. Yeah, I mostly just sleep on it in couch form. A bit cramped, but really not too bad."

"I bet your grandfather appreciates the company," I said.

"He does," Nick admitted with a nod. "But it's better for me as well. I was staying with some friends from high school. They have a loft over a bar downtown. Lots of space and they would have been happy to have me forever, but it was really not a good fit for me."

"Too loud?" I guessed.

"That," he agreed. "But also..." He seemed to think twice about what he was going to say, scrunching up his face as if the words he was holding back pained him.

"Tell me," I prompted.

"They're my friends, and I love them, but they're just sort of coasting through life. Minimum effort, you know? They're perfectly content, but after my time in the military, I like having a schedule. I like getting things done, going to bed knowing something got accomplished. Not that I'm doing anything so awesomely important or anything."

"I get you," I said.

He looked over at me again, and my stupid stomach did that flip over thing again. "I believe you do," he said.

He wouldn't stop looking at me, even when I dropped my own eyes.

Then, to my relief, we finally reached Mrs. Olson's house.

Well, mansion really.

"Shall we?" I said, and we jogged up her front walk to her door. Summit Avenue was an eclectic mix of architecture. The charm school was an American Queen Anne style, while the condos where Nick and his grandfather lived were modernist of all things. Mrs. Olson's place was Richardsonian Romanesque. Not a style I liked; it was built to tower over you and make you feel small, and presumably make the owners feel bigger.

As forceful as Mrs. Olson's personality was, she didn't really seem like she fit in that house. But back in 1927, I had met her grandfather, William Brown, the man who had had the house built to his specifications. It was almost like I could feel his spirit inhabiting the place, looming over me. Especially standing there on the front porch where I had met him before.

I half expected him to answer the door. My hands twisted together as I listened for footsteps to approach after Nick rang the bell. But the house was silent. Nick rang again, leaning on the button a bit. Then he knocked.

He had a very official, police officer on duty sort of knock. I kind of admired it.

But still, there was no answer. Nick turned to me with a shrug. The worried lines were back on his forehead.

"Mrs. Olson?" I called, cupping my hands over my eyes as I tried to peer into the little decorative window in the door. I couldn't see a thing. No lights were on, and the day outside was too overcast to be of any use illuminating the hallway.

"Maybe a different window," I said, jumping off the porch and into the plantings that I realized too late had been put under the windows as a thief deterrent.

"Careful," Nick said.

"Yeah, it's a bit scratchy," I said. That first jump in had left red streaks all over my hands, and it took a bit of time to free my clothes from every snagging thorn. But I pushed my way closer to the house rather than back towards the yard where Nick was watching me.

"Nothing," I said, over and over again as I worked my way from window to window.

The back door was, not surprisingly, locked. Nick tried knocking and calling for Mrs. Olson, but there was still no answer.

I lifted the lid on the trash bin at the bottom of the back stairs. There was only one neatly tied bag at the bottom of the bin. I had no idea how much Mrs. Olson usually threw away, or even when the pickup was.

"Now what?" I said as I let the lid close with a bang.

Nick ran a hand through his dark blond hair. "I guess we wait a few days and try again."

"That's it?"

"Do you have a better idea?" he asked, not remotely sarcastically.

"Maybe one of the windows is open," I said, although I hadn't noticed any on my way around the house.

"We can't go in there without some sort of reason," Nick said.

"Why not?" I asked.

"The law?" he said. His expression was part amused, part suspicious, like he wasn't sure if I was kidding or not.

"Of course," I said.

"There's got to be a way to find out who her next of kin is," Nick was saying as I edged up close to another of the windows and tried once more to catch a glimpse of anything inside. "If they don't live close enough to let us in, maybe we could just get permission..."

I cupped my hands around my eyes, but it didn't help. Nothing inside but darkness.

The darkness bothered me. It felt too intense. Like it was a physical thing. I kind of wanted to see what would happen if I pointed my wand at it.

Probably nothing. Anyway, I didn't remotely want to do that with Nick standing right behind me.

Still, the feeling that something was deeply, profoundly wrong was so strong it was making my whole body tingle.

It wasn't as strong as my compulsion feelings. I wasn't being driven to enter Mrs. Olson's house. But I knew in my bones that I had to get inside.

"Amanda?" Nick called, worried.

"Something is not right," I said as I left the window to stand by him at the bottom of the back steps. "It's not right. It didn't feel right the day I came back, but I ignored that. It feels even more wrong now. Really, really wrong."

"I agree," Nick said, although I doubted he was feeling the same thing I was.

"We have to do something," I said.

For a moment, I could see that he was tempted. He looked up at the back door, and I could see him doing a sort of mental calculation of what it would take to kick that door in.

Then he shook his head as if coming back to his senses. "I'm going to find her next of kin," he said.

"Can't we just pretend we heard something suspicious? Like a scream or something?" I asked. I was hugging my hoodie close around me—it felt like the air had dropped about a dozen degrees since we started knocking on the door—and he could tell I was completely serious. Serious, and worried, and upset.

But, even so, he wasn't a rule-breaking kind of guy.

"I'm going to talk to Nelson. Even without next of kin, he should be able to get some patrol officers to do a welfare check," he said. I remembered Nelson. He was already a cop. He had been kind enough when Cynthia had died on our back step, but he would be even more by the rules than Nick, I knew.

A fat drop of rain splatted right in the middle of my face, rain that was just on the verge of becoming ice.

Then the sky opened up, and we were both pelted with sleet.

"I'm going back to my apartment to call," Nick said, pulling his hood up over his head. "I'll let you know the minute I hear anything, okay?"

I nodded, pulling up my own hood.

But the minute I burst in the back door of the charm school, I was yelling for Brianna and Sophie. The only two people who would possibly take my gut feeling seriously.

CHAPTER 7

The rain had completed its transition to icy sleet, but I could no longer feel it. Brianna easily expanded her invisible umbrella charm to cover the three of us as we walked back to Mrs. Olson's front door.

I had expected to have to do some convincing, but apparently the look on my face had made any explanations totally unnecessary. I had found Sophie first, making herself a cup of espresso in the kitchen, and before I could utter a word she had yelled for Brianna, taking my arm and leading me to the front door where we met Brianna running down from the library.

"It might be nothing," I said as we huddled together on the uneven concrete of her front step. Back in 1927, it had been pristine, but the decades between had been hard on it and it badly needed replacing.

"I trust your feelings," Sophie said.

"What feeling did you have?" Brianna asked.

I shrugged. "Just a sense of wrongness. Do you feel it?"

They both closed their eyes for a moment. Brianna opened hers first with a sad little shake of her head. Then Sophie opened hers a moment later to give us both a pensive look.

"It is something," she said. "I'm not sure what, but the normal flow of magic around this house is... snagged."

"We need to go inside," Brianna said and knocked briskly on the door.

"No one will answer," I said. Sophie glanced at one of the windows, then looked at me. "I couldn't see anything before, but it's darker outside now."

"No need," Brianna said. "I can get us inside. But brace yourselves. I'm going to have to drop the umbrella charm."

Sophie and I pulled our hoods up. I thought I had braced myself, but the sudden pelting of cold rain was icy enough to make me gasp out loud. Sophie, less accustomed to the cold being from Louisiana, made an even more miserable sort of sound.

Brianna said a word that sounded like Latin, then tapped her wand on the front door. We heard the lock inside sliding open, then the doorknob turned, and the door swung away from us, disappearing into the darkness of the front hall.

"Hello?" I called as I stepped inside, hugging myself to stop my shivering. There was a smell in the air, sweet but putrid. I didn't like it.

Sophie stepped in beside me, and we took a few cautious steps further into the front hall. I blinked as my eyes adjusted to the grayish light barely passing through grimy windows. The hall was dominated by a grand staircase, a balcony on the second floor overlooking the checked tile floor we were standing on.

I could imagine party guests gathered here, drinks and hors d'oeuvres in hand, all laughing and talking, then falling silent as someone appeared at the top of those stairs to make their grand entrance.

I just couldn't imagine that person being Mr. Brown. I had never met his wife. She had died long before we visited him in 1927, but I had rather gotten the impression she had never lived in this house. Perhaps he had intended to marry again and had never gotten around to it.

I doubted Mrs. Olson had ever gotten much use out of the grand staircase, either. The intricate carvings in the wood of the balustrade were coated with dust to the point where I couldn't figure out what they were supposed to even represent. The largest in the central position looked like some kind of coat of arms, a shield with fleur-de-lis topped with a knights' visored helmet and with dramatic billows of ribbon behind all of it.

Sophie and I both jumped as the door behind us shut with a slam.

"Sorry," Brianna said. "The wind took it."

"What's that sound?" Sophie asked. At first, I didn't hear anything except the patter of rain against the windows, but then I heard a voice speaking in a low drone.

"Where's it coming from?" I asked in a whisper. We all looked around, each of us tipping our heads like dogs as we tried to catch the almost inaudible voice.

Brianna pointed to a closed door at the left side of the hall, and I nodded. That was where I thought it was coming from, as well.

Brianna clutched her wand and advanced on the door. Sophie took out her own wand and held it at the ready. I patted my back pocket and felt my wand still there, jutting up the back of my hoodie. But I didn't pull it out.

Brianna slowly turned the doorknob until it could go no further, then pulled the door open enough for the three of us to peek inside.

The room beyond looked much like the parlor back at the charm school. Old but well-maintained furniture gathered around a fireplace that didn't look like it ever saw much use. The light in the room had an electric glow to it and flickered in random patterns of dimness and brightness.

A television. The voice was still too low for me to make out the words, but the rhythm of the speech was that of a newscaster.

"Hello?" I called, and Brianna and Sophie both jumped. I pointed to one of the chairs with its back to us, the one that seemed to be blocking us from seeing the television. It was a high-backed chair, the kind where the sides formed wings to give a sense of privacy. A hand-made lace doily was draped over the top of it.

And above the doily, we could just see the very top of someone's head, gray hair floating untidily around it.

The head of someone who didn't turn when I had spoken.

Brianna and Sophie advanced with their wands, moving away from each other to circle on opposite sides of the chair. I followed behind. I had my hands up like a martial artist waiting for their opponent to make the first move.

Not that I know any martial arts. I've seen a few movies, and I had a friend in high school who had studied karate for years and used to try to teach me some of his moves, but I knew I didn't remember any of it.

With or without a wand, I wasn't going to be any use in a fight.

Brianna came around the chair first. Her whole body slumped as she lowered her wand, then tucked it away.

"Oh, poor Mrs. Olson," Sophie said, putting her own wand away.

Then I finally saw her, and sickeningly realized where the smell was coming from. She must have been in that chair for some time.

She must have been dead before I'd even returned from Iowa.

"We should have come sooner," I said. "I noticed she wasn't around the day I got back. And I had the feeling of wrongness then too. I should have made you come over with me then. I got distracted."

"This isn't your fault," Brianna said. "She was likely already dead, anyway. There was nothing any of us could have done."

"Something is very wrong here," Sophie said. I was about to agree when a sudden feeling like the most intense cramps of my entire life had me doubled over. I reached out for support, catching one of the arms of Mrs. Olson's chair.

"Amanda!" Brianna cried.

"I'm okay," I said through gritted teeth.

"You really don't look okay," Sophie said. "We should get you back home."

"No, it's not me," I said. "I mean, there's nothing wrong with me." I took a few more breaths as the last of the crampiness released its hold. "It was that feeling of wrongness. It's like it decided all of a sudden to physically manifest itself."

"But we found what's wrong, didn't we?" Sophie asked.

"We should call the police," Brianna said.

"I think Nick was already doing that," I said, and they both looked up at me with a start.

"You were here with Nick?" Brianna asked.

"The police are coming?" Sophie demanded at the same time, albeit more shrilly.

"He was worried about Mrs. Olson too," I said. "But he didn't think we should go in without probable cause or someone's permission."

"So you got us instead," Sophie concluded.

"Not just to help me break in," I said. "Maybe this is something we have to solve again."

"I don't know, Amanda," Brianna said. "She looks like she sat down to watch one of her programs and just passed away peacefully."

I glanced at Linda Olson's face. She had already started to decay, but even tuning that out I had to agree with Brianna. She looked like she had died in her sleep of natural causes.

I cried out as another cramp rippled through me. Sophie caught my arm, and I could hear her voice as if across a great distance, telling me to just breathe.

The cramp faded, and I found myself clutching Sophie's arm and taking deep controlled breaths with her as if one of us was a doula and the other was giving birth.

"We should get you home," Brianna said. "Maybe even to a doctor."

"No," I said, taking another deep breath. "I think I triggered it by thinking there was nothing wrong. It didn't like that."

Brianna was frowning at me. "I've never heard anything like what you're describing. I would really like to give you an examination. It might be what you say, or it might be something like appendicitis, in which case we should really get you to a doctor STAT."

I was about to object again, but Sophie spoke first. "How would you tell the difference?" she asked.

"I have a spell," Brianna said. "I created it on my own as a way of examining the insides of animal specimens without having to kill them or slice them open. It makes a ghost image like a CT scan. I can see anomalies, both magical and mundane. Although the mundane ones are outside of my field of knowledge."

"Do it," Sophie said, pointing at Mrs. Olson.

"Yes, do it to her," I agreed.

Brianna looked startled, then intrigued. She took out her wand and started speaking in a voice I'd never heard come out of her before. It was like two voices at once, a lilting high one and a rumbling bass one that spoke slower.

I saw this video on YouTube once of a Mongolian throat singer. I had been blown away at the thought that any human throat could make that kind of sound. It had been so eerie, yet cool.

The sound coming out of Brianna was beyond even that. The lilting voice had a heartbreaking melancholy to it that brought tears to my eyes. The lower tone echoed through my chest in a low rumble that made me feel uneasy, like something was hovering over me, just behind me, just out of sight, but if I turned to look, it would be gone.

Then Brianna made a flicking motion with her wand and a silvery light drew up out of Mrs. Olson's body. An exact replica of her body floated up out of her. Brianna made some more flicks of her wand, and the ghostly Mrs. Olson straightened out to lie flat on her back, floating five feet off the floor.

"Woah," Sophie said. "That's amazing, Bree."

But Brianna's attention was focused on the form she had created. It looked like a ghostly form of Mrs. Olson's naked body, but I found if I changed the focus of my eyes, I could see inside of her.

"Look at her heart," Brianna said. "See all the color concentrated there? It looks like it really was just a heart attack. Poor dear."

She raised her wand to dismiss the ghost, but I caught her wrist before she could.

"Do you see something else?" she asked, but I didn't answer. I really didn't know what it was I was looking at. All the structures of Mrs. Olson's body, I suppose, although I was less confident than Brianna that I knew normal from abnormal.

But the twinge in my gut was guiding me. When my gaze swept the wrong way, it would threaten to cramp again, and I would move my eyes back, but too far that direction would bring the cramp as well. Eventually, I found what I was apparently meant to see.

"What is that?" I asked, lifting a hand over the floating form to point to the corner of Mrs. Olson's eye.

Brianna and Sophie both leaned in, eyes narrowing as they too adjusted their focus. It was like when you were looking at the 3D image of a boat that had a picture of a shark hidden within it. You had to relax, stop trying, and all at once you would just see it.

"Wow," Sophie said. "What is that?"

"I'm not sure," Brianna said, moving around to get a closer look.

"I'm sure," I said, my gaze sweeping up and down the short silver channel from the corner of her eye to the center of her brain. "It's proof of murder."

CHAPTER 8

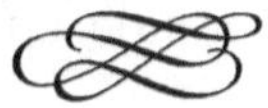

We stared at that ghostly form until the spell began to fade. The floating simulacrum of Mrs. Olson's body sank to the floor, silvery bits of it gathering up and dispersing as if being blown away by a wind we couldn't feel.

Then it was gone.

Brianna looked around for a light switch, gave up and pointed her wand at the light fixture above us, commanding it to turn on. It had a warm, yellow glow, not particularly bright, but enough for the three of us to lean in close around Mrs. Olson's body.

"I don't see any sign of it from here," Brianna said, putting her face far closer to the corpse than I would have done, what with the thick smell of it so much stronger when you got too close. "Not a puncture, not even a drop of blood. There might have been tears, I suppose, but after so many days..."

"What do we do now?" Sophie asked.

"We have to call the police," I said.

"I meant before that," Sophie said.

"Before that?"

"We're agreed that this seems like something magical, aren't we?" Sophie asked.

"I don't know," Brianna said. "It's definitely something that might be missed, especially if no one sees any reason to do an autopsy, but it also seems like something that could be done by anyone."

"Any psychopath with a really long needle," I said.

"So she wasn't killed by magic," Sophie said. "But magic was somehow involved. The patterns around this house are odd."

"But you never looked at them before today," Brianna said. "Maybe they always were. Maybe it's a side effect of being so close to our house."

"Then there's Amanda's gut," Sophie said.

"My gut definitely says this is on us," I agreed.

"We can't hide this," Brianna said. "We can't risk looking like we tried to cover up something."

"They're going to be suspicious," Sophie said. "First Cynthia, then Mrs. Olson. Twice inside of a month, we three have found ourselves standing over a dead body."

"They knew Cynthia wasn't us," Brianna said. "And they'll think this is natural causes."

"Do we want them too?" I asked. Brianna gave me a puzzled look. "I mean, I totally agree with Sophie that we have to investigate this, but the police have resources we don't have. We should make sure they are using them."

"How are we going to do that?" Sophie asked. "We can't tell them what we saw. Or get Brianna to show it to them again."

"No," I agreed.

"Hold on," Brianna said, patting the pockets of her skirt and then her sweater before pulling out a small glass vial.

I decided not to ask why she had such a thing in her pocket, or if she always had one in there, just in case.

"I'm going to take a sample from the inside of that channel," Brianna said, making little circles with the end of her wand at the corner of Mrs. Olson's eye. "Tears and blood. It might tell me something. But I'll leave just a little behind at the corner of her eye. A tear of blood. I think that should be enough to make the medical examiner look further."

"Good idea," I said. "You know a lot of useful spells."

"I've been studying," Brianna said, her cheeks coloring even as she focused all of her attention on the stream of fluid she was directing into the vial. She stoppered it with a little cork and slipped it away, back inside her pocket.

"In Miss Zenobia's library?" I asked.

"Yes. It's a never-ending sequence of rabbit holes. Fascinating rabbit holes, but a distraction from my proper studies all the same," Brianna said.

"I'm sorry," I said. "I know how important your studies are to you."

"They are," she agreed. "But our responsibility to guard the time portal is more important."

"It's hard now because we're new," Sophie said. "It will get easier when we get more used to it. Miss Zenobia managed to do it all alone while also running a secret school within a school. How time-consuming must that have been?"

"Yes," Brianna said, but she looked like she was really thinking about something else as she twiddled with the vial in her pocket.

"Why don't you take that sample back to the lab and do your testing? I'll call the police and wait here for them," Sophie said.

"What are we going to tell them?" I asked.

Sophie shrugged. "We found a door unlocked, maybe?"

"No, Nick and I checked less than an hour ago," I said. "That's the problem. We had no reason to break in."

"Maybe we could pretend we heard something?" Sophie said.

"But what? She's clearly been gone for days," I said.

"It's really a shame we can't just tell them the truth," Brianna said.

"Maybe it's best that we can't," Sophie said glumly. "Just in case this turns out to be partly our fault."

"Our fault?" I asked.

"Maybe something slipped through when we were struggling to hold the bridge across time stable," Sophie said.

"I don't think so," Brianna said, at the same moment I said, "that could scarcely be blamed on us."

The three of us fell silent for a long moment. In some distant corner of the house, a clock ticked.

"I'll break a window," I said at last. "I'll say I found it after Nick left and decided to investigate. I found the body and called Sophie. Then Sophie calls the police."

"What about me?" Brianna asked.

"You were never here," I said. "You need to be figuring out what you have in that vial, not answering the same questions that Sophie and I can handle without you."

"Yes, go," Sophie said. "We'll take care of this end of it."

Brianna nodded and left the room. A moment later, the front door banged shut.

"Which window?" Sophie asked, looking around the room.

"None of these," I said. "Nick and I walked around the whole house. It would have to be something believable that we missed."

"Second floor?" Sophie said.

"Good idea," I said. We went out to the grand hall and climbed the stairs. I found myself walking on my tiptoes, anxious not to make a sound that might disturb the house. As if it were a living thing. As if it might be grieving or upset over the loss of its one remaining resident. I couldn't tell if Sophie was feeling the same way. She always glided softly and lightly everywhere she walked.

"The bathroom, I think," Sophie said, looking in each doorway until she found it.

"Why the bathroom?" I asked.

"It's a smaller window, tucked against the slope of the back porch roof," Sophie said. "Easy to miss if you were looking from the ground, and yet a prowler could get to it pretty easily by pulling up onto the porch roof."

"Perfect," I said, just as we found the room. The window was narrow but tall. A person could slip through easily enough if they turned sideways. I started to pick up the heaviest object in the room, a cast iron magazine holder filled with glossy fashion magazines that were surprisingly current given Mrs. Olson's rather mundane choice in clothing.

But a thought hit me. "Is this too perfect?"

"What do you mean?" Sophie asked.

"Assuming they don't somehow figure out that we did this," I said, not sure that was even a safe assumption, "is this giving them a bunch of clues that will lead them to nothing but a dead end? I mean, how did the murderer get out of the house? Some more subtle escape route they'll never look for if we give them a really obvious one?"

Sophie bit her lip, eyebrows furrowing in thought. "This wasn't random," she said. "All of her stuff is still here, so it wasn't a robbery gone wrong. It doesn't seem very serial killer-y."

"Okay," I said, prompting her to continue.

"Brianna is going to figure out what she can about how Mrs. Olson was killed," Sophie said. "And unless it really was magic, the medical examiner will figure that out, too. What we really need the police for is finding the list of suspects. Who benefits from Mrs. Olson being dead? They'll compile that list either way, right? I would have to guess that would be routine. How that person got in and out shouldn't matter."

"Unless this whole thing from beginning to end is all magic-related, in which case it doesn't really matter either way. It's not their jurisdiction," I said. But I set the magazine rack down with a sigh. "Is there a way we can break the window and make it look like an accident?"

"Maybe," Sophie said, leaning in close to the window and looking around.

"I'll say I saw the window and was worried," I said. "I know it's technically breaking and entering. I guess if they want to charge me with that, I'll go with it. I mean, we did do it. But only one of us gets in trouble that way."

"There's a tree," Sophie said.

"Not terribly near," I said, leaning over her shoulder to also gaze out the quickly fogging window.

"Stand back," Sophie said, taking out her wand. She summoned a rush of wind, and the gentle patter of rain became like a hail of bullets. Then a branch broke from the tree, spiraling towards us with such speed I shrieked out loud. It burst through the window like a spear, sending showers of glass and rain throughout the bathroom. I threw up my arms to protect my face but realized none of the glass was quite touching me. I looked down at my hands and saw them glowing faintly. The glow faded even as I looked at it.

I looked up at Sophie.

"Yeah, I've been practicing a few things too," she said, tucking her wand away. "So this is where you came in. And you went downstairs and found Mrs. Olson in front of the television, and then you called me."

She took out her cell phone and gave me one last questioning look. I gave her a nod, and she stepped out into the hallway before dialing 911.

I don't think they really believed my story. In truth, I didn't try very hard to sell it. I leaned hard on the one true thing I could tell them: that I had a bad feeling about Mrs. Olson that wasn't going away and I was very, very worried.

Sophie pointed out the bloody teardrop to every officer who came into the room until they kicked her out of the crime scene.

By the time they were done asking me every question backwards and forwards, it had stopped raining, but the sunset was a distant memory. The front of the house was a bustle of activity as police officers gathered evidence and prepared to move Mrs. Olson's body to the medical examiner's van waiting at the curb. Sophie and I ducked out the back door instead. A tall fence divided Mrs. Olson's backyard from ours, and there was no gate, but that wouldn't be much of a problem for Sophie, I was sure.

I was just tucking the detective's card into my pocket when I noticed someone standing at the bottom of the back porch stairs. At first, I thought it was another officer, searching the trashcan much as I had done, but when Sophie's prattle about our dinner options abruptly ground to a halt, I looked more carefully and realized it was Nick.

He had his hands in his pockets and gave Sophie a polite nod, but when his eyes met mine, I knew he was upset with me. If he were my parent, he'd be telling me he wasn't angry, so much as disappointed. But everyone knew that was worse.

"There was a window," I said, taking a few steps off the porch to point up at it.

"There wasn't, before," he said.

"I didn't notice it at first either," I said, but words failed me as he just glared at me. It was probably the darkness or the yellowish tone to the light over Mrs. Olson's back porch, but I would swear the green of his eyes had darkened. I couldn't lie to those eyes. "Something here was wrong. We both felt it."

"I was working on it," Nick said. "The right way. By the rules."

"I know," I said. "I'm sorry. I just couldn't be that patient. I had to know."

"Nelson tells me she had been dead for some time," Nick said. "You didn't help anything by breaking in."

"I know," I said, and Sophie hissed in a breath. Now they were both pissed at me, one for lying and one for telling the truth.

"I should have listened to my gut when I first felt like something was wrong," I said. "I regret that. I don't regret this."

Nick looked like he wanted to argue, like he wanted to say so much at once that he locked up the gears of his brain.

In the end, he just gave me a curt nod and said, "understood." Then he turned his back to me and walked away.

I kind of wish he would have yelled at me instead.

CHAPTER 9

One of the strangest things about living in Miss Zenobia Weekes' Charm School for Exceptional Young Ladies was how Mr. Trevor was very seldom seen, and yet always knew just what we needed. Or, more accurately, just what we were about to need.

Case in point: when Sophie and I came in the house, we were both starving but knew there wouldn't be time to cook anything. We really needed to check in with Brianna in the cellar right away and see how her tests were going.

So we weren't exactly surprised to see a plate stacked high with turkey sandwiches still warm enough to emit little curls of steam. Not surprised, but deeply grateful. Sophie scooped up the platter, and I grabbed napkins and plates, and we carried it all through the solarium and out the back door, then down the steep wooden steps to the cellar.

"We have food," Sophie announced as we followed the glow of light to the little alcove filled with alchemy equipment. A couple of Brianna's boxes from the dining room had found their way down here, and an array of more modern lab equipment was interspersed with the Bunsen burners and hand-blown glass beakers.

"Just a minute," Brianna said in that faraway voice that said the

61

number of brain cells she was devoting to talking to us was somewhat few. Sophie set the platter down on the woodworking bench, and I handed her one of the plates and napkins.

"So, that was awkward back there," she said as she daintily bit into one of the sandwiches.

"You mean with Nick?" I asked.

"I mean with Nick," she said. Her eyes were twinkling at me with good humor.

"Yeah, I think I might have ruined that," I said, not quite able to keep my tone as light as hers. "Not that I know what it was, or if it was even a thing."

"Oh, hey," Sophie said, switching from teasing to real concern. "I'm sure it's not so bad as all that."

"He was pretty mad," I said.

"He'll come around," Sophie said. "Just give him a little time."

"All this stuff I can't explain. That's always going to be a barrier," I said. Sophie nodded in a way that felt like something more than mere empathy. But then, we were all in the same witchy boat.

A timer beeped, and Brianna pushed a button on a little machine, peering at the screen for a moment before walking over to where Sophie and I were leaning on the woodworking bench and eating.

"Wash your hands first," I said as a distracted Brianna tried reaching for a sandwich. She looked down at her hand, the tips of her fingers stained with some sort of chemical that, while not Mrs. Olson's blood, was probably something a lot less safe to ingest. She headed to the sink in the corner.

"Anything?" Sophie asked as Brianna scrubbed her hands dry on a clean white towel, then took the plate I held out for her.

"I've done everything I can think of," she said. "No sign of magic."

"What signs would there be?" I asked.

"Magical weapons, either specially forged or spelled mundane weapons, leave traces of the magic behind. There is no sign of that here," Brianna said. "It definitely wasn't just some sort of piercing spell; that would have glowed so brightly we would have seen it when we were standing around her. I even checked for magical poisons, either injected or coated on the blade, but nothing."

"You've ruled out a lot of things. That has to help," I said. Brianna just shrugged, still unhappy. "Sophie, you sensed something around the house," I prompted.

Sophie nodded, swallowing the last bite of sandwich before answering. "I'm not sure what that was, how long ago the warping happened, let alone what caused it. It might have been there for decades. Or it could be related to the murder; I don't really know."

"Brianna, do you have any way of studying it?" I asked. "One of your machines or something?"

"Maybe," Brianna said doubtfully.

"What about you?" Sophie said to me.

"I don't think I'll see a thing," I said.

"No, that feeling you had," Sophie said.

"I've had lots of feelings," I said. Sophie was about to respond, but I held up a hand. "I'm not being dismissive, really. I do have lots of feelings. The one I know the best is the compulsion one, the one I have to obey. This wasn't that. Then there was the sense of wrongness that wouldn't go away until I got inside that house. Personally, I don't think that was anything remotely magical. I was just worried."

"Are you sure?" Sophie asked. "I mean, when you were feeling it, it was really strong, right? But you kept setting it aside, forgetting about it."

"Don't remind me. I wish I hadn't set it aside," I said.

"That's just it. Maybe it wasn't really you choosing to ignore a thing," Sophie said.

"Being busy is no excuse," I said, but Brianna was shaking her head at me as well.

"I see what Sophie is saying. If your worry was rooted in some sense of the magic warping that Sophie noticed, the fact that you kept forgetting about it might have been a sort of counterspell."

I liked the idea. Perhaps too much. I shook my head. "No, I don't think it was that. It didn't feel like being under a spell. I just got wrapped up in other things."

"Being under a spell doesn't necessarily feel like being under a spell," Sophie said.

"We can't prove it one way or another now, but let's keep it in mind," Brianna said. "What about that sick feeling you had?"

"Yes, that's new," I said. "That definitely felt like magic, like an outside force directing me. Or, I guess, the opposite of directing me? It would hit me whenever I thought that Mrs. Olson's death was natural causes or not something we should investigate."

"A spell to keep you on a path," Sophie mused.

"More like one to keep me from going off it," I said. "I don't see the path, so there's no way I can avoid going off it. But, boy, does it let me know when I do."

"Hopefully that's over now that we're committed to investigating," Brianna said.

"Hopefully," I agreed.

We finished off the plate of sandwiches, and Brianna went back to the alchemy station to clean up and put away the equipment. There was still some fluid left in the vial that stood alone in a test tube rack, canted to one side in a way that looked forlorn.

"The tissue in that vial," I said, then fell silent again.

"Yes?" Brianna asked as she wiped her microscope down with an alcohol swab, then pulled the plastic cover over it.

"I know I didn't grasp even a fraction of the reading you assigned to me," I said, "but there was a thing in there about sympathetic magic."

"The tissue in the vial shares a bond with Mrs. Olson," Brianna said, nodding. "Both her body and her spirit. But summoning spirits is a bad business. We don't really understand where they go, and they are often angry to be yanked back here. Angry and not cooperative."

"Oh," I said. "I hadn't even been thinking of that." Summoning spirits of the dead? I guess it sounded like a witchy sort of thing to do, but not one I was anxious to try. "No, I was just thinking. It also touched the weapon, right? Which is why you ran all the tests for magic."

"All of them," Brianna said. "There's nothing else to look for, I'm sure of it."

"So it was a mundane weapon. No magic involved at all," I said. "But there's still a link to the tissue in the vial."

"Oh," Sophie said as if she'd jumped ahead of my rambling explanation. "That might work."

"A locator spell?" Brianna said, also jumping ahead of me. "I think that would work. But what if it directs us to something inside Mrs. Olson's house? That's a crime scene now. We can't go back in there."

"If only we'd thought of this before we called the police," Sophie said.

"Maybe it's not in the house," I said. "Maybe it's in the yard, or still in the murderer's possession."

"It could lead us to the murder," Brianna said.

"And then we could lead the police to both somehow," I said. "Can you do it?"

"Not a problem," Brianna said. She took out her wand and paused a moment to call the words to mind. Then she raised the wand and began that double-throated chant until a silvery light rose up out of the vial and streaked like a comet across the cellar.

"Follow it!" Sophie yelled, nimbly leaping the stool set close to the wood stove and racing for the stairs. Brianna made some motions with her wand as if trying to reel the light back to her, but it was already out of sight, leaving nothing but a silvery glow that was rapidly fading from the top of the stairs.

I ran after Sophie, Brianna close behind me. We burst out into the yard. The soles of my Converse sneakers slid over the wet grass, and I nearly fell back onto my butt, but Sophie danced ahead as if she hung from wires.

"There it goes!" she cried, pointing up into the sky from where she stood in the center of the orchard. Brianna spoke a word and gestured with her wand.

"Did you catch it?" I asked.

"No," Brianna said after a moment's silent assessment. "It's gone."

"Gone where? Over the wall?" I asked.

"No," Brianna said, looking around us and twitching her wand. I knew she was seeing something I didn't, which was deeply annoying.

"It couldn't have gone straight up into the sky. That doesn't make any sense," I said. "Maybe we should go out to a wide open area and try it again. It didn't go towards Mrs. Olson's house, so it must be leading us to the murderer."

Sophie walked back to us, her face grave. "Did you see that?" she asked.

"Yes," Brianna said.

"No," I said, hating how sullen I sounded, but hating more the fact that in a world filled with magic, I was worse than blind.

"But I don't understand," Brianna said. "We didn't let anything pass."

"We didn't let any*one* pass," Sophie said. "But a thing? A small thing?"

Brianna pushed past Sophie to examine each of her brass detectors. "I should still have known," she said when apparently none of them told her anything.

"Mrs. Olson was murdered days ago," I said. "Before I got back from Iowa. Maybe days before."

"Maybe those first few days, when everything was so overwhelming," Sophie said as Brianna continued to shake her head.

"Brianna, we have to face facts," Sophie said. "Whatever weapon was used to kill Mrs. Olson, the police are never going to find it. Because somehow, whether it was originally from there or from our time or from some other time altogether, the murder weapon is in 1927."

Sophie and I looked at Brianna, but she just kept shaking her head.

"If someone had punched through the fabric of the portal, I would have known," she said.

"But if the weapon was small—" I started to say.

"I would still have known," Brianna said. "If a mosquito tried to pass through, I would know."

"Okay," I conceded. "Well, then perhaps the locator spell went awry."

Brianna was angry enough to make eye contact with me, to give me a truly withering look. "My spell did not go awry."

"Then I guess you're at a logical impasse," I said, letting my annoyance show. "You figure out which of your premises doesn't hold true."

I regretted those words even before they were out of my mouth, but even more when Brianna's face started to crumple.

"Hey," Sophie said. She moved as if to give Brianna a hug, but at Brianna's instinctive flinch she quickly changed the motion to a bare two fingertips on the back of Brianna's wrist: a tap of comfort. "It won't hurt to just go back to 1927 and take a look around."

"It really doesn't make any sense," I said. "Who in 1927 would even have a motive? Mrs. Olson wasn't even alive then."

"It won't hurt to take a look," Sophie said, giving me a hard look.

"No, it wouldn't hurt," I said. "Except, it's the middle of the night."

"She's right," Brianna said, and Sophie and I exchanged a glance and a shrug. We had no idea which of us she was agreeing with and which she was speaking to. "We'll go in the morning and try the spell again on the other side of the time bridge. In the meantime, I'm going back to the library. I need to think some things through."

"Okay, but be sure to get at least a little sleep," I said.

"I'll go with her," Sophie said. "I actually have a thing or two I want to look up myself about the warping I felt. You coming in?"

"I'm going to grab the dishes first," I said, and went back down into the cellar. I gathered up the platter and plates and dirty napkins and carried them up the stairs, then set them on the grass as I pulled the heavy cellar doors shut over the stairwell and clicked the padlock shut.

I started to head up the porch steps, but a sudden urge struck me to try again to sense the magic I knew was all around the backyard and particularly the orchard. I set the platter and plates near the door and pulled out my wand.

It felt warm in my hand, warmer even than my body heat. Did that mean something?

I walked out to the center of the orchard, where all of Sophie's dancing meditations always began and ended, and tipped my head back to look up into the sky. A tattered wisp of cloud blew past the crescent moon, and a few cold stars twinkled down at me, but I saw nothing more. I closed my eyes, raising my wand up high, rising myself up on tiptoes. I didn't know any words or movements, nothing I could do to make the vision come except wishing. So I did that, with all my heart and soul.

Then I opened my eyes.

Another wisp of cloud was rolling in over the moon. Just that, nothing else.

Then I heard a sound behind me, the grit of a paving stone grinding under a sneakered foot, then someone clearing their throat. I whipped my wand behind my back, stuffing it desperately in the general direction of my back pocket but being thwarted by the folds of my hoodie.

"Hey," Nick said as he stepped into view.

"Um, hey?" I managed, my throat suddenly painfully dry.

Crap. Had he just seen me flailing around while I gazed up at the sky like a crazy person?

CHAPTER 10

*H*e just stood there for the longest time, hands deep in his pockets and looking pretty much everywhere but at me. Which was just as well, as I was still fumbling at the back of my hoodie. Finally, I got it pulled up enough to tuck my wand in underneath it and smoothed it back down just as he finally looked my way.

"I know it's late, but I thought I heard someone moving around back here, and I thought I'd take the chance it was you," he said.

"It's me," I said. Now that I had my wand hidden, my hands were suddenly acutely aware that they had nothing in particular to do. I touched my hair and realized that I had done nothing with it since getting soaked in the rain earlier and it probably looked a fright. It could have matted down, it could have frizzed up, but I was pretty sure it had managed both in random patches all around my head.

I pulled up my hood.

"You wanted to talk to me?" I finally managed to ask.

"Yeah," he said, but then he lapsed back into that maddening silence.

"About the case?" I prompted.

"Yeah. No. Kinda." He seemed to be frustrating even himself as he pulled his hands out of his pockets and ran them through his hair. "It's chilly out here. Can we go inside? For just a minute," he quickly amended.

"Sure," I said. "Tea?"

"Lovely," he said, in the tone of someone very eager to agree to anything at all. I picked up the stack of plates, and he rushed to open the screen door for me. If he thought it was odd that I had been out in the yard at nearly midnight with a stack of plates and napkins, he said nothing about it.

I put the dishes in the sink, then made sure there was water in the kettle before switching it on. I thought Nick would sit at the table, but perhaps he truly did only intend to stay for a minute, as he just leaned against the counter and watched me take mugs out of the cupboard and put a bag of chamomile in each.

Clearly he wanted to say a thing, and clearly, he couldn't figure out a way to just get the words out. I tried sneaking little looks at him out of the corner of my eye, but I could get no sense of his emotional state beyond being deeply conflicted. He had a lot of feelings roiling around.

I knew how he felt.

"Look, I wanted to say I'm sorry," I said, and he blinked at me in surprise.

"You wanted to say you're sorry? To me?" he said.

"Yes. I said I didn't regret what I did, and in the main, I don't, but I do regret that I wasn't honest with you," I said. "I knew before you even left that I'd be getting into the house, no matter what."

"I see," he said. Again, I couldn't get a read on what he was thinking, which was frustrating. I was usually pretty good at anticipating people's wants and needs. It was a skill that had come in really handy in the diner. I know it's not something most people brag about, but I had been a really good server.

But now? With Nick? Nothing. I couldn't even tell you if he was the kind of guy who would have a ton of instructions for the cook on just how he wanted his burger done, or if he'd ask me what I thought was good and go with that.

I leaned in, looking him right in the eyes. Those green eyes with flecks of gold. But I looked past that, deeper.

"What?" he asked, standing back from the counter.

"Medium, all the veggie toppings, but definitely extra bacon. And cheddar, not American," I said.

"What's that?" he asked.

"How you like your burger," I said as the kettle beeped and I filled both mugs with the hot water.

"How I like my..." he blinked. "What are we talking about?"

"Nothing," I said, handing him his tea.

"Suddenly I'm hungry," he said.

"We might have some sandwiches in the fridge," I said. I turned to open the door, but he caught my arm and spun me back.

"No, that's fine," he said, setting his tea down but not letting go of my arm. "I think I lost my thread, why I was here."

"Sorry," I said.

"Stop that," he said with a mock intensity that was covering for a genuine wish for me to stop apologizing.

"Okay," I said, looking down at the hand on my arm. He seemed to notice it as well and quickly let me go.

"I came here to apologize to you," he said. "If you could stop spinning my head around for a minute."

"Okay," I said, taking a sip from my tea that was still far too hot. I pressed the back of my hand to my burned bottom lip and put the cup back down. "It's really not necessary," I said.

"It is," he said. "I shouldn't have gotten so pissy with you."

"I earned that," I said.

"Well, maybe," he conceded. "But, I know I get a little hardcore with following the rules sometimes. My buddies in Afghanistan called me Boy Scout, and it wasn't really from affection."

"There are worse things than following the rules all the time," I said.

"All the time? Blindly?" he countered.

"But that's not what you did," I said. "Well, I didn't know you in Afghanistan, but today that's not what you did. You were doing the same thing I was, getting someone to see if Mrs. Olson was okay. And like you said, they were already on their way when Sophie called them, so really you did the right thing."

"I should have done the right thing sooner," he said, pulling at his hair a bit too aggressively.

I remembered what Brianna had said, about how there might have been a spell preventing me from checking on Mrs. Olson. It still didn't feel to me like that was what had happened to me, but looking at Nick and his misplaced guilt, I really, really wished there was some way I could tell him it was all a spell.

"I don't think there was anything either of us could have done," I said. "I do think it was all over very fast."

"Yes, that's what the medical examiner said," Nick said. He sniffed, then took a sip of his tea.

"You talked to the medical examiner?" I said. "They did an autopsy already?"

"No, just an initial examination," Nick said. "They are doing a full autopsy in the morning with a screen for poisons, but she told us she didn't expect to find any. It looked like the object entered the corner of Mrs. Olson's eye and pierced straight through to the center of her brain. Quick and painless, and she may have been asleep when it happened, as there was no sign of a struggle."

"I guess that's good," I said. "As much as any of this can be good."

"Yes," Nick agreed.

I took another sip of my tea. "Did you ever locate any next of kin?" I asked as conversationally as I could.

"No," he said. "I did some searching and so did Nelson. Her husband died when her son was twelve, and then her son died during Operation Desert Shield. She never remarried, and she was the only child of an only child."

"How terribly lonely," I said. "No wonder she was always in the yard trying to strike up conversations."

Nick gave a little laugh. "Sorry," he said at my quizzical look. "That's just so you. Linda was out there every day grilling all the passersby and enforcing imaginary neighborhood rules, but you see it as a lonely woman chatting with potential friends."

"Didn't you see it that way?"

"Yes," he said, sobering. "Yes, I did. I always made a point to talk with her when I came by. She could be grumpy, but she could also be kind. She was sharp and knew everything about the neighborhood. I'm really going to miss her."

This time, I was the one to reach out and catch his arm, giving it a reassuring squeeze. He covered my hand in his and gave me a little smile.

"So no family at all? Not even distant cousins?" I said, as he turned his attention back to the remains of his tea.

"Not exactly family," he said. "But there is someone she has a sort of legal connection with. Nelson spoke with her briefly and is going to meet with her tomorrow."

"Suspect?" I asked.

"Oh, I shouldn't think so," Nick said. "Linda Olson's name was unfamiliar to her, and he had to go over the legal connection a few times before she agreed that it could be a real thing."

"What's the legal connection? Am I allowed to ask, that is?"

"Linda died with no will, and her late husband had never had one either, nor her father. The binding document now will be her grandfather's will, it seems."

"Her grandfather… William Brown?" I said.

"Oh, you know the name?" Nick asked, frankly surprised.

"Yes, um," I cast about for a logical reason for me to know this factoid. "He was the original builder of the house."

"That's right," Nick said. "At any rate, his will left everything to Linda, his only grandchild, but had stipulated that if she died, everything would go to some other entirely unrelated person. I don't know if it will even be legally binding after all this time, but Nelson tracked down the person who would be the beneficiary, the grandchild of the original beneficiary. Yeah, who knows?"

He drained the last of his tea, then dropped the tea bag into the bucket where we kept things destined for the compost pile as if he too lived in the house and was intimate with all of its day-to-day affairs. Then he rinsed the mug and set it near the sink.

I watched him do all this, my mind racing as I knew I was running out of time. There had to be some casual way to get the beneficiary's name out of him, the current one or the ancestor. Either would do. But how?

Nick was drying his hands on the dishtowel, and I could almost hear the whisper of the last few grains of sand in the metaphorical hourglass slipping away.

Not that it had worked in the yard, but once more I found myself just wishing really hard. Wishing he would just say the name, or that maybe even it would just pop into my head if I stared at him long enough.

He looked up at me, startled at the intensity of the gaze I was throwing at him.

"You okay?"

"Sorry. Just tired, I guess," I said, blinking.

Well, that had been just as useless as I had expected.

"Yeah, I should get out of your hair. I have class in the morning anyway," he said.

He turned to walk to the back door, and I trailed along behind him, trying not to feel like a failure. I hadn't really had a shot at success, anyway.

Nick opened the back door, then the screen door, before turning to look back at me. I thought he was just going to say good night, but an odd look came over his face.

"What is it?" I asked.

"Hm?" he said as if from far away, then blinked and the strange look was gone. "Wow, don't know what that was. I guess I'm tired too, just blanking out on you."

"It is late," I said.

"Yeah," he said, but then hesitated again before leaving. "Look, it's not likely to come up since Nelson is talking to her tomorrow, but just in case she gets curious and comes around, maybe you could keep an eye out?"

"For the beneficiary?" I said.

"Yeah. I doubt she will, but just in case," he said.

"Sure," I said and mustered a smile. "How will I know her?"

"I expect she'd be the only woman likely to turn up," he said. "But she has dark hair and dark eyes. In the photo, I saw of her online, her hair was long and pulled back with a pair of little combs, but it looked like a picture from college so that might not be accurate anymore."

"Okay," I said. Then, just as he was about to turn away again. "Her name?"

"Oh, duh, that would help," he said with a grin. "Mina Fox. Her name is Mina Fox. See you tomorrow sometime?"

He was smiling at me expectantly, and I forced my mouth to turn up at the corners, to form the words, "sure, tomorrow."

Then I closed the door, leaning back against it and wrapping my arms around myself, hugging myself tight.

The name had not been familiar to me, but the sounds it had made when he had spoken it out loud had sent a chill through my body, a chill that lingered still somewhere in my bone marrow.

Just who was Mina Fox?

CHAPTER 11

"What was that name again?" Sophie asked me.

"Mina Fox," I said.

Sophie looked at me, then looked at Brianna. Brianna shrugged.

I had to admit that I wasn't feeling the chill anymore, either. Maybe it was just that it was daylight now, although a dim, early morning sun that barely illuminated more than the floor in the attic space where I had found Sophie and Brianna already choosing out 1927 outfits.

"I'm just thinking, maybe we should go talk to her first before we go back in time," I said.

"Why? Because you felt a thing?" Sophie asked. She wasn't being mean.

"She has motive," I said.

"But you said that Nick said that Nelson said that she didn't know the name Linda Olson when he—Nelson—called her," Brianna said, ticking names off on her fingers.

"She could have been faking," Sophie said.

"Which we could get a read on if we just go meet her," I said. "Even if she doesn't know anything, she can give us information about her ancestor that was named in the will."

"That is smart," Sophie agreed. "It will give us something to go on besides just the locator spell. Not that the locator spell won't work or anything."

Brianna shrugged. "More leads are always good things. I'll go tell Mr. Trevor we need the car."

"Hold on," I said before she could head for the stairs. "I had another question. A magic thing."

"Shoot," Brianna said, although the way she shifted her weight from foot to foot said she was anxious to go.

"Can you make something happen just by wishing it?" I asked, ignoring the heat in my cheeks. After a mostly sleepless night debating whether or not that was a stupid question, I had decided not to ask. Up until just a second ago, that is.

"Like what?" Sophie asked. "Like, 'I wish I had a slice of death by chocolate cake' and boom! One appears?"

"I don't think it works that way," Brianna said with a frown. "The laws of physics, specifically conservation of energy—"

"No, not like that," I said. "Last night when I stayed in the yard, I was trying to make myself see what I saw before when I came back from 1927 on my own. I wanted to see the time bridge."

"Did you?" Brianna asked, brightening.

"No, that didn't work," I said. "But then I tried it again when Nick was going to leave last night. I wanted to know the name of the person in the will, but he wasn't telling me, and I didn't want to pry by asking. So I just wished it, really hard. At first, I didn't think it had worked, but then he stopped just before leaving, and he had this weird look on his face. And then he told me her name."

"The name that gave you chills," Sophie said.

"Did. Doesn't now," I said, my eyes on Brianna.

"I don't know," Brianna said. "There are old legends about witches with incredible power, but finding the truth in a legend... I don't know, Amanda. I'd have to have a lot of evidence to believe that. A lot."

"Which doesn't mean we don't believe you," Sophie rushed to add.

"No, that makes sense," I said. "It's probably just a coincidence. He came over to tell me things. That was probably one of them. It just felt weird. In the moment."

"It was a long, weird day," Sophie said.

"Pay attention to that sort of thing," Brianna said. "Keep a log. Not just when you think you make things happen, but every time you have one of your feelings or compulsions or anything like that. Maybe we can find a pattern. In the meantime, I'll go find Mr. Trevor."

As usual, when we needed him, he was very easy to find. Scarcely ten minutes later, we were climbing into his immaculately clean town car. Brianna had searched for the name Mina Fox online and was typing an address into the car's navigation system.

We probably could have walked it; I realized as Mr. Trevor drove us halfway down the length of Summit Avenue before turning off onto Snelling Avenue to drive past Macalester College. I had walked this far before, although on that day I was killing time and today was promising to be a busy one. Mr. Trevor turned again onto a residential street, then stopped in front of a cute brick home with gingerbread trim sitting comfortably back from the road, tucked under the wide arms of an elm tree.

"I'll wait here, shall I?" Mr. Trevor said, already pulling a paperback book out of his pocket.

"We won't be long. Thanks, Mr. Trevor," Brianna said, looking back over her shoulder to check for traffic before hopping out of the passenger door.

Sophie and I echoed our thanks as we scrambled out of the back seat. It was another chill, overcast day; October was feeling a lot more like November, with Halloween still more than a week away.

Brianna rang the doorbell, and we heard a woman's voice tell us she was coming.

"Did you call her?" I asked Brianna.

"No, just found the address," she answered.

"Maybe she's expecting Nelson," Sophie said, but before I could say anything, the door was swinging open.

At first, I thought we had the wrong house. Nick had said to look for a brown-haired woman with brown eyes, but this woman's hair was all silver and starting to thin and had a brittle look to it. But the eyes behind the thick lenses of her glasses were a deep chocolate brown, and the combs that held back the thinning wisps of her hair were tortoiseshell.

I tried to speak, but the name wouldn't pass my lips.

"Mina Fox?" Brianna said instead.

"Yes, dear?" the woman answered.

"That's who you are?" Brianna persisted.

"Yes. Are you from the lawyer's office?" she asked politely.

"Not exactly," Brianna said.

"We live next door to Mrs. Linda Olson," I said.

"Oh. Oh, dear," she said, then fumbled at the screen door handle. "Please, come in. Come in. Oh, I'm so sorry for your loss."

"We only knew her a short time," I admitted as we all stepped into the house. There was no front hall; the door opened directly into the living room that was somehow overstuffed despite only containing a sofa, two chairs, and a coffee table in between. Behind the sofa was an old cabinet that would probably be a valuable antique if in better shape. It was a nice art déco piece that looked like it had been left out in the rain more than once.

"I'm afraid I never knew her at all," Mina Fox was saying, waiting for Brianna to clear the doorway so she could close the door against the chill. "It's most peculiar. She had no family at all?"

"Not that we knew of," I said.

"Most peculiar," Mina said again. "Can I offer you coffee or tea?"

"No, thank you," I said. "We don't want to take up a lot of your time. You're meeting with lawyers today?"

"Yes, and the police are sending someone to ask me some questions as well," she said, settling herself on one of the poufy chairs then waving her hands until they took seats around her, Sophie in the other chair and Brianna and I on the sofa.

"Really, it's almost embarrassing. I don't have any need for the money. My own family left me enough to be comfortable, and at 71 with no children of my own, I don't need much more than to be comfortable."

"Pardon us for asking, but do you know how you ended up being named in the will?" I asked.

"Oh, it wasn't me. At least, not directly. No, it was my grandmother named in the late Mrs. Olson's grandfather's will."

"William Brown," I said. "We know a bit about him. Historically."

"Oh, yes?" Mina said.

"Self-made millionaire," I said. "He had the house on Summit Avenue built to his specifications, and it's been in the family ever since. But he wasn't from here originally. He was from out east."

"Is that so?" Mina said.

"Yes," I said. "Do you know how your grandmother knew him? Was that also out east?"

Mina drew in a long breath, then let it out slowly. Then she summoned the smile back to her lips. "I beg your pardon. I'm not accustomed to discussing family matters with strangers."

"I'm sorry," I said. I realized I had been sitting forward as if awaiting the most salacious of gossip and forced myself to sit back against the overstuffed back of the couch.

"No, this is a unique circumstance," Mina said. "And it's not so much that I don't like to talk about it as that there isn't very much that I know. My grandmother died when I was quite young, and my mother never did like talking about her. My mother was an almost stereotypical fifties housewife, so proper and sensible. Always being mindful of what the neighbors might think. When my grandmother was still alive, she never came to visit. We always went to see her. I almost got the sense that this was a secret from my father. I think she might have told him that her family was all dead. I don't really know for sure. She never liked to talk about it, and since my grandmother died when I was young, it didn't really matter."

"Your grandmother was eccentric, then?" Sophie asked with an indulging smile.

"Eccentric? Yes, you could call her that," Mina said with a faraway look on her face. "She always had the most gorgeous things. Spanish shawls and golden trinkets and so much jewelry. I rather wonder where it all went when she passed."

"Gifts from suitors?" I asked, trying to imagine a reason she would be named in William Brown's will. I remembered the single conversation I had had with him. He didn't seem the type to be nostalgic for a past love.

"Suitors?" Mina said as if pondering the word. "I never thought of that. Perhaps some of them were. Even in old age, she was a stunning woman. More than just her looks; when she stepped into a room, she instantly had everyone's attention. What's the phrase? Magnetic personality."

"Perhaps she was friends with Mr. Brown, then?" I asked.

"Oh, perhaps," Mina said, but she didn't sound convinced.

"Not a lover, not a friend," I said, ticking off my fingers. "Did they maybe have a business connection?"

"That's what I've been assuming," Mina said. "My grandmother had many important business connections."

"Was she an investor?" I asked.

"Some sort of deal maker?" Sophie added.

"Consultant?" Brianna offered. Mina turned to Brianna with a grin.

"Consultant. Perhaps 'advisor' is the better word?" Mina said.

Mina was still looking at Brianna with that smile on her face, which left me free to examine Mina's face in detail. She seemed sincere. Her eyes matched her facial expression, and I saw no twitches, tics or tells to hint that she might be lying.

And yet, I felt like she might be toying with us. Maybe not in a diabolical way. More like she was having a bit of fun at our expense.

"What's the best word for it?" Sophie asked, still giving Mina her most winning smile.

"Medium," Mina said with a triumphant grin. "My grandmother was a medium, a fortuneteller, a communer with spirits. And she made many men rich, far richer than the gifts she had left at the end of her life would indicate. That's gratitude for you. Not that I'm complaining. I've managed to live quite nicely on the trust fund she left behind for me."

There was a sound from outside of two more cars pulling close to the curb to park behind Mr. Trevor.

"You have other visitors," I said, getting to my feet. "We won't take up any more of your time."

"It was very nice to meet you," Mina said, getting up from her own chair to walk us to the door. She was very spry for 71. More than just a lack of aching joints or unsteady gait; she moved like a trained athlete. But then, living off a trust fund as she did, she had probably always had time enough for exercise, for an active hobby or two.

"Thank you for your time," Sophie said. "If you should ever need anything, we live right next door to the house you're inheriting."

"Oh, that's very sweet of you, but I can't imagine myself knocking about in such a large, empty space," Mina said. "Perhaps the historical society would appreciate it? But honestly, I can't see how that decades-old will could still be legally binding. I doubt I'll see a penny. Which is just fine with me."

"Oh, Ms. Fox? One last thing?" I asked as she opened the front door to let us out and the police officers and lawyers in.

"Yes, dear?" she asked.

"What was your grandmother's name? Just for curiosity's sake."

"Her name was Cora. Cora Fox," Mina said.

"Thank you."

I was relieved to see that neither of the police officers waiting on the front porch was Nelson, although one of them quirked an eyebrow in a way that made me suspect that our descriptions had gotten around.

Even in a time when the charm school was long closed, its reputation for being filled with exceptional young ladies in the forgotten past, we made a threesome that was easy to describe and hard to forget. And we were already gaining a bit of a reputation all on our own.

"Well?" Mr. Trevor asked as he climbed into the car.

"Home," Brianna said.

"Then to 1927," Sophie added. "We have some leads to follow up."

CHAPTER 12

*B*rianna didn't seem to feel the cold as she moved from birdbath to sundial to clothesline, waving her wand and staring into the air as if it contained some sort of readout that only she could see. Which it probably did. She had put a wool coat on over her day dress but hadn't bothered with any of the buttons, just let it swing around her in the chill breeze as she worked.

I, on the other hand, was freezing. I had chosen a sweater and skirt set and was also wearing a wool coat, but I missed modern technology's wind-blocking materials.

Sophie finally came out to join us, swinging a beaded handbag in one hand and toying with her long necklace with the other. She saw me watching her as she came down the porch steps and gave me a little wink, then adjusted the cloche on her head. Like Brianna, she wore her coat open, but in her case, I knew it was a deliberate choice to show off the stunning dress beneath. The slinky material was a deep, rich red, almost too lustrous for daytime, but she pulled it off.

"You like it?" she asked, giving a little turn.

"It's you," I said diplomatically.

"You have nicer things in your closet, you know," she said. "Although the blue of your sweater does match your eyes nicely."

"Girls my size are not what the creators of the dropped waist look had in mind," I said.

"Nonsense," Sophie said.

"Are we ready?" Brianna asked.

"Ready," Sophie said, grasping her handbag more firmly as she started dancing in slow turns around the orchard.

I didn't bother trying to see the magic. I was hoping it would be like a Zen thing, where I could succeed only when I let the effort go. But I still really wanted to see something, which is probably why I didn't.

October 1927 was bright and sunny, and very hot.

"My goodness," I said, unbuttoning my coat and slipping it off my shoulders. "It's like 80."

"Yes, how odd," Brianna said, pulling her notebook out of her pocket and writing furiously. "Both points are fixed in time and move in conjunction; I should be able to create a device that can tell us the weather before we cross over. Sort of a magical barometer," she said, flipping a page and resting the book against her thigh before sketching the rough outlines of what she was thinking of.

"Also, we could just consult the almanac in the library," Sophie said.

"No, what Brianna is thinking looks way cooler," I said.

"So, what are we doing first?" Sophie asked.

"Let's find Cora Fox first," I said. "It seems like that might take longer than the locator spell. I don't suppose there's any sort of address directory we could consult?"

"If she's even listed in such a thing," Sophie said.

"She must advertise," I said.

"I think mediums tended to find work by word of mouth," Brianna said, slipping her notebook into her dress pocket and only then taking her coat off. "Let's leave our coats in the house and take a look around. Maybe there's a directory in the library, or a local paper or something that might have a hint of where she could be."

Just like every other time we had gone back to 1927, we saw no sign of Miss Zenobia or any of the charm school students. Brianna had some theories as to why this was, involving time paradoxes and the like. We knew the school was active at the time—the neighbors saw other students coming and going—but we never did.

When we went into the kitchen, there were three teacups sitting around the table, some half-drunk but all still gently steaming, as if someone had heard us coming and just got up and walked away before we came in.

We left our coats hanging from the hooks near the front door, then went up to the second floor to the library. In 2018, Mr. Trevor brought the newspapers upstairs in the morning and left them out on a table near the glass doors that led out to the front porch. He had never traveled back in time himself, but someone in 1927 had the same job. Sophie and I started turning pages of newsprint while Brianna went deeper into the library in search of a directory.

"Nothing in mine," I said as I turned the last page.

"Nor mine," Sophie said, picking up her paper to look more closely at the classifieds, then shook her head. "Not a thing."

"There is a directory, but she's not in it," Brianna said. "Should we try the locator spell instead?"

"I have a thought," Sophie said. "Mediums were really con artists, right? Maybe the criminal underground is the way to go."

"You mean Otto?" I asked.

"He seemed like he had his fingers in a lot of pies," Sophie said.

"Yes," I agreed. "If he doesn't know where to find her, he certainly knows how to find out."

"So, what are we going to do?" Brianna asked. "Just walk down there? Alone?"

"Sure," Sophie shrugged.

"But what if he's not there?" Brianna asked.

"Then we ask," Sophie said.

"It does seem like a rough neighborhood, even in the middle of the day," I said, and Brianna looked relieved that I understood her.

"Everyone knows we're from the school and respects us, remember?" Sophie said.

"I don't know if we know that for sure," Brianna said.

"Maybe we should find Edward first," I said.

"It's the middle of the workday," Sophie said. She picked up one of the newspapers to double check the date in the header. "Yes, it's a Thursday here. And we don't know where he lives or where he works."

"But we know who might," I said. "Let's see if Coco is around."

"Again, we have a middle of the school day problem," Sophie said, but the three of us went outside, anyway.

I hadn't made any particular wish to find Coco, and I hadn't had one of my feelings, but I wasn't entirely surprised when she was coming down her front steps just as we were coming down ours. She had an apple in her hand and took an enormous bite out of it as she gave us a happy wave.

"Hello, Coco!" I called. "I'm sure you're on your way back to school after lunch, but can we talk to you for a moment?"

"Sure," Coco said around a mouthful of apple and trotted over to stand under the tree with us. She swallowed, then grinned up at us. "Aren't you going to ask me why I'm home in the middle of the day?"

"Don't you come home every day for lunch?" Sophie asked.

"No. I wish I did. Our food is so much nicer," Coco said, taking another bite from the apple. "No, we were supposed to have stew today. You know what they do on stew day, don't you? They just use up all the rotten leftover bits from earlier in the week. So nasty! So do you know what my friend Carol and I did? We hid all the spoons. Every last one of them. They had to send us all home! If only we could sneak them all out of the school and bury them down by the river, we'd never have to eat their food again."

"Somehow I doubt that's going to work," Sophie said, but she couldn't help the grin that spread across her face.

"Coco," I said. "We're looking for Edward. Do you know where we can find him?"

"He's not here," Coco said.

"But do you know where he works? Or where he lives?"

Coco gave a disinterested shrug and continued to munch at her apple.

"Coco," Brianna said. "Do you know when he was here last?"

Coco wiped her sleeve across her mouth. "Yesterday afternoon. My sister Ivy had some guests before dinner. He was one of them."

"Thank you, Coco," Brianna said.

"You should get on to school before you're late," Sophie said.

Coco rolled her eyes but started walking backwards away from us. "I'll see you around?"

"Certainly," I agreed, and she turned and started running down the street.

I turned to Brianna. "How does knowing he was here yesterday help us?" I asked.

"I'm guessing a spell," Sophie said, and Brianna nodded. She looked around carefully to be sure no one was about before taking out her wand. She waved it over the grass in a low sweeping motion and murmured some words under her breath.

"Nice," Sophie said, looking at the grass all around her.

"What?" I asked, not seeing anything.

"Footprints," Sophie said. "Glowing footprints."

"Too many footprints," Brianna frowned. "Okay, I think I can narrow it down. If I alter the fourth syllable, I'll just be looking for the paths left by men. And if I stress the end bit a touch more, it should skew to younger men."

She waved her wand and whispered again as Sophie continued to turn this way and that, watching the grass around her.

"Four trails," Sophie said.

"I don't think I can modify it any better," Brianna said.

"Four's not so bad," I said. "Considering all of Ivy's suitors, this is probably the best you're going to get."

"This one," Sophie said, pointing towards the sidewalk.

"Why that one?" Brianna asked. "It's no different from the others."

"It feels like him," Sophie said with complete confidence that she immediately undercut by giving a little shrug. "I mean, we have to start somewhere."

"Okay," Brianna agreed.

I was a sweaty mess pretty much the minute we started walking. Brianna's dress had long sleeves, but the fabric was still fairly light, and she seemed comfortable. Sophie's dress was sleeveless; she was cool in both senses of the word. But my sweater was as bad a choice here as it had been back home when it had failed to keep out the cold.

Luckily, we didn't have far to walk. The footsteps led us towards the cathedral, then down a cobblestoned side street called Maiden's Lane. There were a few houses, but mostly the buildings here were carriage houses for the mansions built on the ridge where the slope was too steep for such things.

Of course, most of the inhabitants of Summit Avenue had cars now, not carriages, but the brick structures remained. And many looked like they had apartments over them.

The trail of footprints I couldn't see led about halfway down the narrow road before taking a sudden turn to the right, up a narrow flight of stairs to one of those little apartments.

"Do they end here?" I asked as Sophie started up the stairs.

"At the door," Brianna said. "Why?"

"What if he's not home? You don't see any path leading to where he might work?"

"No, just the one set of prints," Brianna said.

Sophie was already knocking on the door. She knocked again a moment later as Brianna and I looked up at the dingy windows. They were so small and so filthy it was impossible to see even a hint of anything on the other side. He could be standing there now staring back out at us, and we'd never know.

Sophie knocked a third time, then gave us a shrug as she started back down the stairs.

"Now what?" I said.

"Time for Plan B," Sophie said, fanning herself with a fan that matched her dress. I was going to have to set some time aside to really explore what my own closets contained.

"Was Plan B the locator spell or going to see Otto ourselves?" I asked.

Sophie had been looking up at the apartment windows. She glanced back over her shoulder at me, but whatever words she had been about to utter died on her lips, replaced with a sly smile.

"Ladies," a voice said, and I turned to see Edward standing right behind me in the middle of the road. "It's lovely to see you again, although I'm curious how you knew where I live, and why you came here if you're looking for Otto?"

CHAPTER 13

$\mathcal{I}$ might have been caught off guard and left a little tongue-tied, but Sophie was as smooth as ever. Edward readily believed that Coco had given us directions and was amused by an abbreviated accounting of the missing spoons. Then she had him explaining all about his work in an office downtown and agreeing to forego his planned lunch at home for a hot meal off the street if he would agree to escort us back to Otto's hideaway.

"I know a man who sells the best hot sausages," Edward said as we walked into town. "He's from Bavaria originally. Old family recipe, he says. And he serves them up in a hard roll that's worth the cost all in itself."

"Well, it's our treat since you're helping us out," Sophie said.

"It does sound fantastic," I said, and my stomach growled aloud just at the mental image. I was embellishing a lot from what he had told us, mostly because I was incredibly hungry and nothing beats Bavarian sausage.

"I haven't seen you around lately," Edward said, and I realized Sophie and Brianna had fallen a few paces behind us, deep in a whispered conversation of their own. His suit lacked a jacket, and I suspected he had left it behind when he had headed out for lunch. He had rolled up the sleeves of his white shirt, and I wondered how he maintained such nice muscle tone while trapped in a desk job.

"I've been away," I said. "I had to go back to Iowa to take care of some things, but I'm here to stay now."

"That's good," he said, then cleared his throat nervously. Was I making him nervous?

"How are things with Ivy?" I asked, and he moaned.

"Oh, the same," he said at my questioning look. "We exchange letters, and it's like we're both thinking and feeling the same things, but then I go to see her, and there are all these other fellows who seem like they feel the same way, like she's the perfect one for them. But it's just as well if she's not ready to choose one of us. I'm hoping to get a promotion soon that will really increase my prospects."

"Yes, I suppose it would be difficult to make a marriage proposal to a girl like Ivy. She would have a lot of expectations," I said as diplomatically as I could.

"Yes," Edward said and cleared his throat again. "Her father has taken a shine to me, which is terrific. He sees how serious I am and how hard I work. And Ivy and Coco are his only children. No sons. So whoever Ivy marries will probably be the one to take over his business someday. Which is why I really hope I get this promotion. I'll have more responsibilities. That just has to impress him."

"And if you could afford to move into a nicer apartment?" I said with a smile.

"Definitely a nice bonus," he said, smiling back at me.

He wasn't wrong about the sausage.

When we finally reached the cellar under the former beer hall that was Otto's headquarters, the normally clammy coolness of the air was positively delicious on my overheated skin. This time Edward didn't have us wait outside the final inner circle of crates, just rapped loudly on the corner of one as we walked into the walled-off space.

Otto was at the table that sat under the bare bulb that hung from the low ceiling. He appeared to be examining some sort of hand-drawn map of a building, making a notation with a stub of a pencil, but when he glanced up and saw the four of us coming in, he tossed the stub aside and came around the table with a big grin on his face.

"How lovely to see you all again. Miss Sophie," he said, taking her hand and pressing a kiss to the back of it. Sophie slipped it out of his grasp when I think he would have preferred to hold it a bit longer, folding her arms as she looked around the room. The usual collection of stolen items and boxes of illegal alcohol were strewn around the space, stacked up high against the crate walls.

But Otto himself was looking very different. Gone were the clothes of a dock worker. Now he wore a tailored suit complete with shining watch chain, and his thick blond hair was slicked back in what was a stylish haircut in either of our eras. His blue eyes were all over Sophie, but eventually he spared a glance at the rest of us.

"What can I help you all with today?" Otto asked, rubbing his hands together.

"We're looking for someone," Sophie said. "A medium by the name of Cora Fox? She might be doing business under another name."

"Cora Fox," Otto said, his voice brimming with admiration. "Ah, she's a fine one. Not as fine as you, to be sure, but a real shrewd operator."

"So she is a con artist," I said.

"She's a medium," Otto said with a shrug. "She has her own network of sources, but there's a bit of overlap between her network and mine. Not the sort of situation I usually let stand. No man can serve two masters and all that. But I make an exception for Cora."

"In exchange for a cut of the action?" Edward guessed.

"Hey. I'm a businessman," Otto said. "What are you looking for Cora for?"

"We just need to talk to her about something," I said. "Charm school business."

"Indeed," Otto said, stroking his chin as he regarded me. I didn't think he quite believed me, but he let it go.

"Can you give us her address?" Sophie asked.

"I can do you one better," Otto said with a grin. "I can take you there."

"I'm sure that's not necessary," I said.

"It's too hot to walk so far, and I have a new car I'm just dying to take for a spin," Otto said. "Who wouldn't want to ride around town with such a trio of lovely ladies?"

Before any of us could answer, he went to the gap in the crate wall and shouted for someone named Benny to pull the car around. Then he rolled up the drawing and a few others and stuffed them in a chest, which he locked, putting the little key in the pocket of his waistcoat. Then he took a hat down off a peg and offered Sophie his arm. She seemed to consider it for a moment before sliding her hand around it, letting him walk her back up out of the cellar to the street.

The rest of us trailed a bit further behind.

Knowing that Otto ran some sort of criminal enterprise—one that had taken a recent more successful turn to judge by the dapper suit and bowler hat that had replaced the work clothes and flat hat we had seen him in before—I was in no way surprised to see the car that pulled up in front of us as we waited on the sidewalk. It was just the sort of car gangsters would flee from a robbery in, hanging out the suicide doors and firing Tommy guns at the coppers.

The boy behind the wheel didn't seem old enough to drive, or indeed tall enough to reach the pedals. Otto opened the passenger door, and all but shoved Edward and me into the front seat before opening the back door and helping Sophie glide into the back seat. Brianna was left pretty much to her own devices, climbing in after Otto and tucking herself tightly into her own corner.

There were no seat belts, and the shifter in the middle of the floor compelled me to crush up close against Edward.

"Here," Edward said, sliding his arm out from between us and resting it on the back of the seat, not quite touching my shoulders. "Better?"

"Yes," I said.

He had no right to smell so lovely. Especially not when I, having spent the day perspiring in a wool sweater, definitely did not.

Otto leaned over my shoulder to give Benny directions on where to drive, saw me pressed up against Edward, and gave us both a cheeky wink before sitting back and turning all his attention to Sophie.

"Miss Sophie, you look positively sinful in that dress," Otto said, sliding closer to her.

"Thank you," Sophie said with measured coolness. "What can you tell us about Cora Fox?"

"Ah, Cora," Otto said, that warm tone dripping from his words again. "She is special. Life can't keep Cora Fox down, and believe me; it's tried."

"How so?" Sophie asked.

"Well, she's from New York City originally," he said. "Her mother was from Ireland. She came over alone, no people to look out for her, and she got herself in a bad way pretty much at once. Unwed mothers don't get the plum jobs, to be sure. So Cora grew up no better than Edward or I."

I looked up at Edward, curious what sort of childhood Otto was eluding to, but didn't want to ask and risk missing something Otto said about Cora. Edward noticed me looking up at him and gave me a smile. He had the warmest brown eyes. I could believe Otto had endured a hard-knock childhood, but if Edward had too, I saw no sign of it in the earnest young man pressed up beside me.

"Did Cora also go into service?" Sophie asked.

"No," Otto said with a laugh. "No, that definitely wasn't the life for Cora. She was far too ambitious for that. No, she was determined to marry well and improve her station. Once you meet her, you'll know, but she beats even our Edward here for seeming swanker than she is. Dress her up, put a glass of champagne in her hand, and set her down in the middle of any upper-crust party and no one would ever know that she doesn't belong there."

"I don't know. Those tend to be pretty tight circles," Sophie said.

"Here, maybe, but in New York, things are different," Otto said. I rather doubted he had ever been further away from St. Paul than across the river in Minneapolis, but I didn't interrupt. "She did land a fellow who was all set to marry her, but then he left to fight in the war and never came back to her."

"How sad," Sophie said, and Otto seemed to read more emotion in her tone than I did because he took her hand as if she were in dire need of comfort.

"That's not the saddest bit," he said. "He had fully intended to marry her, but he needed time to bring his father around, who was dead set against the match. So Cora carried on alone. The day she found out he had died in the trenches from some godforsaken disease was the day she found out she was with child."

"That is tragic," Sophie said, gently extracting her hand from his grasp.

"She tried to make a go of it in New York. With no chance of marrying into the wealthy class, she took that same skill set and put it to better use."

"Working as a medium," Sophie guessed.

"Indeed. But eventually, she had worked that market dry and came here to test the waters. So far, she's been doing gangbusters." He fell silent for a moment, and I glanced back to see him giving Sophie another assessing look. "Miss Sophie, that dress was just made for dancing."

"Yes, it was," Sophie said. If it were possible for words to drip with icicles, hers did. "Otto, it's very kind of you to help us out. We appreciate it very much, but I'm afraid anything more than a business relationship between us is quite out of the question."

"Not good enough for you?" he asked with an edge to his voice that sent a chill up my spine.

"Of course that's not it," Sophie said, warming up her tone to an almost friendly level. "You in that suit, in this lovely car, would be a date worthy of any girl. Alas, my heart belongs to another."

"Who is he?" Otto asked.

"No one you know," Sophie assured him. "Just a boy back home in New Orleans. A childhood sweetheart."

"Childhood sweethearts. Always a lovely thing," Otto said begrudgingly. "Still, New Orleans is awfully far away."

"Yes, it is," Sophie said wistfully, and for the first time, it occurred to me that she might not just be telling a story to keep Otto at arm's length. Had she really left someone behind when she'd come to the school?

The car lurched as the boy inexpertly engaged the parking brake. We had reached our destination.

CHAPTER 14

 hadn't been paying attention to where we were going and didn't recognize the neighborhood we were in. The houses were modest but well-maintained, so I guessed the people here were comfortably middle class. The house we were parked in front of had a hedge that framed the walk up to the front porch, then took right angles to form a border between the yard and the sidewalk. It looked a bit shaggy and overgrown, but given the unseasonably warm weather, this wasn't so unusual. Whoever did the gardening would be in leaf raking mode now, counting down the days until snow would need to be shoveled.

"Wait," Sophie said as Otto started up the walk. "I think the three of us should speak to her alone."

"You don't want an introduction first?" Otto asked, looking at Sophie, but still taking a step or two closer to the door.

"I don't think that will be necessary. She'll know who we are," Sophie said.

"Right enough," Otto said and walked back to the car. "I'll wait here to give you a lift back to your house when you're done."

"I'm sure we can find our own way back," I said. "You must be busy, and this might take a while."

"No worries," Otto said, climbing back into the back seat and stretching out. "I can use a little catnap."

"If you're sure," Sophie said. He gave her a wink, then took off his hat, settling back against the far door of the car before setting the hat over his face to block out the sun.

"What about you?" I asked Edward. "Your lunch break must be long past over. And you have that promotion coming; you don't want to compromise that."

"I'll be fine," Edward said. "To be honest, I'm kind of curious what this is all about."

"I'm not sure how much I can even explain," I said, glancing at Sophie and Brianna. It wasn't like when Cynthia had been murdered. That had been pretty easy to convey with the magic bits carefully excised. But this? With all the magic redacted, there wasn't going to be much left to convey.

"Don't pry, Edward," Otto said from beneath his hat. "Charm school business is none of our business."

"You don't have to stay," I said.

"I'll be here," he said and gave me a little nudge to follow Sophie and Brianna up the walk.

Sophie gave her usual brisk knock, which was answered almost at once. The interior of the house was quite dark, and the girl who opened the door seemed to know it, as she took half a step out onto the porch before looking up at us. She was young, younger even than Coco. I would guess nine or ten, so it was a bit of a mystery why she wasn't at school.

Or why she dressed like someone's super religious maiden aunt. Even in the heat, her wool dress was buttoned all the way up her throat, her lovely brown hair pulled back into a bun so severe I was surprised any of it stayed attached to her scalp.

"Yes?" she asked, blinking up at us.

"We're here to see Miss Cora Fox," Sophie said, speaking slowly, as if the girl might have trouble understanding her Creole accent.

"You don't have an appointment. It's only barely one, far too early for appointments," the girl said.

"We're not here for a... seance," Brianna said. "We just have a few questions."

The girl blinked up at us for another long moment. If she was trying to decide whether to let us in or not, I saw no sign of it on her face. But then she nodded and stepped back to let us follow her into a cramped foyer. Straight ahead of us, the narrow hall split into an even narrower staircase going up and a hallway continuing on to the only patch of sunlight I could see. There was a set of French doors to our right which even closed ought to be letting in a little sun, but all I could see through the glass was what appeared to be the back of a cabinet of some sort.

Strange furniture arranging choice.

"You can sit in the parlor," the girl said, waving a hand to the room beyond an open set of French doors to the left. "I'll go upstairs and see if she is receiving." She looked at us again for a long moment, assessing us one at a time, then heaved a sigh. Her next words had clearly been dictated to her on many occasions, and she read them back to us now with all the obvious reluctance a kid of ten could muster. "The spirits occupy her nights, and convening with them is quite exhausting. As such, she is required to rest during the daytime hours, but I shall inquire if she is capable of seeing you at this time." She waved us towards the parlor again, and only once we were all moving in that direction did she turn and head up the stairs.

"Strange kid," I said.

"That sounded like a rehearsed speech," Sophie said as she moved around the room, touching the various knick-knacks. They looked mostly like the sort of cheap knock-offs that a particularly unknowledgeable tourist might accumulate from China, Japan, India, and Egypt. If I had to bet, I'd say Cora had gotten them all in New York City.

"We're not the first people to come during the daytime with questions," I said. "Prior run-ins with the police?" A familiar shape caught my eye, and I slipped around a loveseat to take a closer look at a cabinet in the shadows under the heavily draped front window. Art déco. The sort of thing meant to be passed down over generations.

"Or with truancy officers," Brianna said. "Why isn't that girl in school like Coco?"

"Because she learns at home," said a voice from the doorway, and we turned to see the outline of an imposing woman framed by the French doors. Somehow, a beam of sunshine had penetrated the gloom of the house to light up the foyer behind her, putting her own features into shadow.

Then she plucked a shawl higher up on her shoulders and stepped into the parlor. She was tall, over six feet, I was sure, and statuesque. In another age, she would surely have become a supermodel with her high cheekbones, sultry dark eyes, and thick waves of chestnut hair that hung loosely around her shoulders.

We all stood rather stunned where we were, Sophie on tiptoe as she examined a painting on the wall, Brianna actually with a bronze figure in her hands, me half bent over the cabinet I was sure had been in Mina's living room in 2018. But the woman didn't seem to notice any of us, just slipped past the round table in the center of the room and perched herself on the edge of the largest chair, its tall back higher even than the top of her head.

Sophie was the first of us to recover her wits. "We have some questions," she said, but the woman spread out her hands, indicating the other chairs clustered around the little table.

"Please, sit," she said. "I am Cora Fox. I will answer any questions you might have, but I have some questions of my own first."

"What sort of questions?" Sophie asked as we each took a chair.

"Not questions for you," Cora said and held out a hand for me. I was puzzled at first and had the urge to flinch back, but she gestured again, and I realized she wanted to see my hand. I held it out, and she turned it over, her warm fingertips tracing over the lines of my palm. "Just as I thought. You are a pawn in a larger game than you know."

"Me?" I all but squeaked.

"Really?" Sophie said, with that level of disdain she was so good at mustering. Cora shot her a quelling look, then reached out for Brianna's hand. Brianna looked like she'd really rather not, but Sophie gave a little shrug, and she relented. Cora gave her palm a more thorough examination than she had mine before saying, "you serve a mistress who is not who you believe she is."

"Me or us?" Brianna asked, her eyes firmly on the floor as she hugged her palm close to her chest. But Cora didn't answer, just turned her attention to Sophie, who held out her palm while somehow managing to look down her nose at the far taller Cora.

"Very interesting," Cora said, tracing line after line across Sophie's palm. She kept doing this without speaking further until even Sophie's patience gave out.

"What is interesting?" she demanded.

"You have a calling," Cora said, finally releasing her hand. "A calling more powerful even than your mistress."

"Are you talking to all three of us?" Brianna asked, but Cora ignored the question. She reached forward, catching the edge of a purple square of silk cloth that was draped over the central table and pulling it away to reveal a crystal ball. A single beam of light from the foyer found it, refracting in the heart of the glass to dazzle all of us gathered around it.

I knew she was a con artist, but I couldn't help respecting her game.

Cora leaned forward, moving her hands around the ball without touching it. Sophie crossed her arms and sat back in her chair. Brianna continued to hug her own hand close and mostly studied the floor. I watched the patterns of the light within the ball but saw nothing unusual. There was a smell like incense but more perfumey. I had smelled it when we first came into the parlor, but it was stronger now. I was pretty sure it was clinging to the clothes Cora wore, trapped in the fringe of her Spanish shawl and the thick folds of her heavy, floor-length skirt.

"Yes," Cora said as she gazed into the glass. "There is another power, more powerful than the one you serve, and through you, that power will find a justice long delayed."

"Okay," Sophie said like an adult playing along with a child's game.

"Do you think that's why we're here today?" I asked, trying to bring the meeting back on track. The smell was making my head swim, and

I had a strong urge to throw open the blackout curtains and let in some sun and fresh air.

Cora looked deeper into her ball before answering me. "No. That's not why you're here. You are here on a terribly mundane matter."

"Yes, I suppose to some murder is terribly mundane," Sophie said.

"Whose murder?" Cora asked, sitting back in her own chair and folding her arms in an imitation of Sophie. I wasn't sure if that was deliberate or not.

"Linda Olson," I said.

"Never heard of her," Cora sniffed.

"Are you sure?" I asked.

"It's a rather common name, so take that as you will," she said, adjusting her shawl around her again.

"Can you explain to us why you are a beneficiary in the will of Mr. William Brown when you are no relation to him?" I asked.

"I will not hear that name spoken, not in my house," Cora said, and real anger flared in her eyes for the briefest of moments.

Then she was slumping back in her chair, pressing the back of her hand to her forehead in the world's most contrived gesture. "I am terribly sorry I can't be of any help to you. If you wish, I'd be happy to try to contact this Linda Olson for you. Spirits, when they are approached with love and friendship, are often eager to help, even with solving their own murders. I've assisted the police in similar manners back in New York City; I can provide you with references if you like. But you really will have to make an appointment for a more appropriate time. If you'll excuse me, I've found this all very draining and must retire. Good day."

She kept that hand over her eyes as she brushed past Sophie and Brianna, then her own daughter, before rushing up the stairs. We heard a door close somewhere out of sight.

"Did that help?" I asked, slumping with my chin on my hand and looking at the light reflecting off of the surface of the crystal ball.

"Not really," Sophie sighed. "But if this was an example of her magic, she doesn't have any. I didn't sense a thing."

"Nor I," Brianna said. "But I didn't like it. What was she talking about?"

"Nonsense," Sophie said, but compared to her usual confidence level, she only seemed to be at about eighty percent.

"But she could be talking about Miss Zenobia, and we do have a calling, although how she could know…"

"It's all nonsense," Sophie said again.

"I know it's not real magic," Brianna said. "It's not even particularly good cold reading. But she seemed to know things she shouldn't. Didn't she?"

I shrugged.

"She knew we were from the charm school," Sophie decided. "She knows the school's reputation. She winged it from there."

"I'm to show you out now," the girl said from the doorway. Sophie and I got to our feet, but Brianna remained where she was, staring hard at the floor.

"You are Cora's daughter?" Brianna asked, just catching the girl's nod with a darting glance. "What's your name?"

"Margery," the girl said guardedly.

"Margery," Brianna said, "do you think your mother can do what she says she does?"

"You mean the palm reading and crystal ball thing or the spirit conjuring?"

"All of it," Brianna said and bit her lip as if steeling her resolve before looking up at the girl, right into her eyes.

"It's all fake," Margery said. "And I can prove it."

CHAPTER 15

We followed Margery back out to the foyer. She put a finger to her lips and motioned for us to wait as she crept halfway up the stairs, head tipped almost comically as she listened for any sounds coming from above. Then she tiptoed back down to us, leading the way down the narrower part of the hallway to the patch of sunlight. The light was coming from a small window over the sink of a kitchen almost as tiny as the one I had grown up with in the one-room apartment back in Iowa.

"She's fast asleep," she told us once we were all inside the cramped space. "She's had her afternoon drop of gin. She'll be out until sundown."

Somehow, I think that probably involved more than a drop. I was pretty sure that even at ten Margery knew that as well, but some things weren't said out loud.

Margery reached past Sophie to push at a door that resisted being opened. Sophie put a hand on it and gave it a hard shove, and it swung free. Margery stumbled but then caught herself, fumbling against the wall until she found the switch for the light.

The room beyond had probably been designed to serve as a dining room. There was an open doorway across from us that led into the front room opposite the parlor. There was some sunlight coming in, but it was mostly blocked. As Sophie and then Brianna squeezed past the door, I followed behind and saw that against every wall from the floor to nearly the level of the ceiling was row after row of what appeared to be library card catalogs. The window was a few inches taller than the cabinet in front of it, grudgingly letting in the barest beam of light diffused through the tree that grew on that side of the house. The entire dining room and front room, nothing but card catalogs with extra loose papers out on tables that filled the middle of the rooms.

"She gets letters and things," Margery said, picking up some of the loose paper from the piles on the table to show us. "Other times it's just rumors from servants that work in the houses, and she writes them down. Every fact on a card. Every card organized into one of those drawers."

Brianna circled the table to peek into the room beyond. The look on her face was simultaneously horrified at the invasion of privacy but also deeply impressed by the structure.

"This must cost a pretty penny," I said, as Margery was looking at us and waiting for one of us to say something.

"I reckon it does," Margery said. "I've seen her pay people, at any rate. But not as much as she makes. Especially folks that lost someone in the war. Sons or brothers or husbands. She can be really convincing. They're generous when they're grateful. And some of them come back a lot. One woman comes every month to talk with her son again."

"How sad," I said, and Margery nodded, but there was a fierceness in her eyes. "It makes you angry?" I guessed.

"It's wrong," she said. "My own father was hurt in the war, although he didn't die until later. I never got to meet him. I miss not knowing him, but he's gone."

"She's never tried to communicate with him for you?" Brianna asked.

"No," Margery said, her voice thick with angry tears.

"Do you wish she would? She must miss him too," I said.

"She doesn't," Margery said, blinking furiously to keep from crying. "She hated him. She never loved him. He was just... rich. He was supposed to marry her, but he came back from France with a different wife."

"I'm sorry you never got to meet him," I said, and pulled her into a tight hug. I don't think she got hugged much. She stiffened in my arms as if she wasn't sure what to do. Then she just melted against me. Still not crying, but I think some of the anger had dissipated.

"I don't see anything here about Miss Zenobia or the school," Brianna said. It looked to me like she was opening drawers at random, but I was sure she wasn't. While I had been talking to Margery, she had mastered Cora Fox's intricate filing system just by glancing at it.

"Wild guesses, then," Sophie said, picking up a letter at random from the table and looking at it before setting it aside. "She doesn't know anything about us."

"What about Mrs. Olson?" I asked.

"Who's Mrs. Olson?" Margery asked, her voice muffled against my sweater.

"Someone who died," I said. "We're trying to figure out who killed her and why."

"And you think my mother knows?" Margery asked, pulling away to look up at me.

"Well, she seems to know a lot," I said.

"Did she tell you she helped solve murders before? Because I'm pretty sure that's not true either," Margery said.

Brianna was trying to catch my eye. She pantomimed something I didn't get at all until she took her wand out and waggled it at me. Then I nodded and pulled Margery back into the kitchen with me.

"Let's get you a cocoa or something," I said, looking around the mostly bare kitchen. The top shelf had a nice array of gin bottles. They looked legit. Illegal. Imported. Expensive.

"No cocoa, but tea," Margery said, then moved past me to get the kettle herself. My plan to comfort her with food was thwarted, but she appeared to find comfort in being useful. That was something.

Sophie stepped into the doorway and leaned one hip against it, ostensibly watching Margery and me, but in actuality, blocking whatever Brianna was doing from view.

"No sugar, but we have a little milk?" Margery said as she set cups on a tray.

"Black is fine," I said, picking up one of the teacups. "These are really lovely."

"Mother uses them for work sometimes," Margery said as she spooned tea into the matching pot.

"She reads tea leaves," I guessed, and Margery nodded. I turned the little cup around in my hands, holding it just by my fingertips. It seemed a shame to use such a delicate piece of art as a vehicle for a beverage. I didn't know how to tell bone china from the regular kind, but when I held it up to the light from the window, I could see my fingers through it. The elegant shape of it was flawless. And I couldn't even imagine the steady hand it would take to paint the little white and blue flowers on it, dotted all around by green leaves. The brush couldn't have had more than a couple of bristles, the lines were so fine.

I was still admiring the cup against the light when a sudden boom of noise made me jump. For an agonizingly endless moment, I was all too aware that I was no longer holding the cup. It had slipped from my startled fingers. It was going to fall. And I was going to have to watch it tumble to the floor and smash to a million pieces all in super slo-mo while my fumbling hands hovered paralyzed before my face.

Then I saw a swoop of red out of the corner of my eye, Sophie dropping low over one foot, then swooping an arm out and up with balletic grace.

But she didn't catch the cup. The wind she was creating swept it up and held it off the ground until her hand reached beneath it.

There was a soft sound as the china touched her outstretched palm, and then my world went back into normal time. Sophie straightened, giving me a relieved look out of the corner of her eye as she reached past me to set the cup back on the tray.

"What was that?" Margery asked. But not with concern or alarm, not about the loud crash that had come from the dining room. No, her voice was full of wonder, and she was looking at Sophie.

"I'm pretty fast," Sophie said. "I'm a trained dancer."

Margery narrowed her eyes, looking from Sophie to me and back again. I knew in my bones that she had seen everything that had just happened, wind and all. She knew more was going on than a trained ballerina catching a cup with her ninja-fast reflexes. She just wasn't sure how to call us out.

But any second now, she was going to find the words.

"Heads up!" Brianna called, and Sophie pressed up tight against my back as Brianna came charging out of the dining room.

In pursuit of a very familiar silver light.

"I thought you were looking for info on Mrs. Olson!" I cried as Brianna followed the light out into the hall. Sophie and I scrambled to run after her.

Margery was hot on our heels. "What was that thing?" she demanded.

None of us was being particularly careful about not waking Cora Fox. But she didn't seem to be waking. Yep, definitely more than a drop of gin had been had.

"Maybe she has a stash of secrets in her bedroom," Sophie said to me as we sprinted up the stairs. Brianna was nowhere in sight, but it wasn't that big of a house. The upstairs was a single short hallway with three doors, only one of which was open.

"What are you doing?" Margery hissed at us. "You can't go in there! That's my room!"

But we did. Brianna was sprawled half under the little bed. She had flipped the edge of a rag rug out of her way, leaving a circle of cleaner floorboards exposed in the center of the dusty floor.

"No!" Margery said, still in a furious whisper. "Get out of my room!"

I looked around, but there was no sign of the silver light. I dropped to a knee to look under the bed just as Brianna started squirming back out from under it. Her hair caught on the springs, and she had to stop with a little cry of pain, shoving a box into my hands so she could use both hands to get her hair free.

"That's mine!" Margery said, lunging for the box.

"We're not taking anything from you," I said, although in truth I had no idea what we were actually doing. "What spell did you do?" I asked Brianna. "I thought you were going to summon information on Mrs. Olson or something."

"I did. There wasn't any," Brianna said, then gave another hiss of pain. Sophie knelt down behind her to help gently tug the strands of red hair out of the springs. "So I did the locator spell from before."

"And it led you here?" I asked. Then I lifted the lid off the box. Margery lunged forward to try to stop me but froze in place as the lid revealed the ball of silvery light hovering inside the box. It flared brightly, then faded away.

"What was that?" Margery asked, once more in a whisper.

I started to reach inside the box, thought better of it, then pulled the sleeve of my sweater down over my hand to use it as a makeshift evidence glove.

Then I lifted out the largest of the items inside the box. Nearly a foot long, sharp and sturdy, and most definitely stained with something that looked like blood.

A hatpin.

CHAPTER 16

argery dropped to her knees on the wadded mass of the rag rug and gave a sad little moan.

"Margery," I said. "What do you know about this?"

"You can't take it. It's mine!" she said, and she was no longer trying to keep her voice low. "That's all I have from my father. The only thing! You can't take it from me."

"Margery," I said, holding it up in the light from the window. It definitely wasn't rust staining the shaft. The red had dried to brown, but had yet to start flaking away. "What have you done?"

"Done?" Margery asked, wiping at her cheeks without quite noticing that she was crying.

"Our friend Mrs. Linda Olson was murdered by an object just this size," I said. "Look, this is clearly blood."

"It isn't!" Margery insisted, but she didn't sound sure. She edged closer to me to get a better look.

"Was it like this the last time you saw it?" I asked.

"No," Margery said, and sniffled hard. "I take good care of it. It's all I have from my real family."

"Does your mother know you have it?" Sophie asked.

"No," Margery said.

"But you never met your father's family. How did you come to have this without her knowing?" Sophie asked, gently probing.

"She knew once," Margery said. "I found it when I was little in a chest in the attic. Back in New York. I kept it forever and ever, but one day she found it in my room, and she got really mad. She threw it away, but that day after she went to bed, I went out to the bin and got it back out. I've been careful since then. She doesn't know I still have it."

"How do you know it's from your father's family?" I asked.

"Look," Margery said and pointed to the head of the pin. I spared a moment to be impressed she had grasped that none of us were touching the thing with our bare hands, then turned the needle around to examine the head of it.

It was far too small of a canvas for such an elaborate portrait, but there on the porcelain knob that covered the top of the pin was a painting that, with a bit of squinting, I could just make out as being a family crest.

Sophie sucked in a breath, and I realized it was one I recognized. It was carved into the woodwork in the hall of Mrs. Olson's house. The family crest of the Brown family.

"Margery, what's your father's name?" I asked.

"Brown," Margery said. "William Brown II. I was supposed to be William Brown III, but I ended up being a girl."

I didn't want to think how many things would have ended up differently if she had been a William instead of a Margery. It would just be angry-making and not helpful.

"Margery," I said. "Someone used this to murder our friend. She was… related to William Brown, Senior."

"I didn't do it," Margery said.

"No, I don't see how you could," I said. "You two never knew each other. But someone who knew about this hatpin knew her."

"But no one knows," Margery said.

"Not even any friends from school or anything?"

She slumped a bit closer to the floor even as Sophie got the last of Brianna's hair free and she was finally able to sit up and look at the pin in my hand. "I don't go to school since we moved here," Margery said miserably.

"No friends?" I asked, my heart breaking a little.

"A few. But I never bring anyone here," Margery said, barely more than a whisper. I could scarcely blame her for that.

"Margery, I want you to close your eyes," Brianna said, moving to kneel in front of the girl so that they were facing each other. Margery sat up a little straighter, then dutifully closed her eyes. "Breathe deeply like this. In and out. In and out." She did, and I found myself taking the same deep breaths. "Good. Now, don't answer right away, but I want you to think back over the last few days. Start with today, then go back to yesterday, and then the day before that, and the day before that. Just imagine all the events of the day from when you woke up until when you went to sleep. See every person who came upstairs or any moment when you were out of the house long enough for someone to come upstairs. Don't answer right away, just let your mind go through all the days, one after another. Did anyone have an opportunity to take this from your safe place, then return it later without you noticing?"

Margery kept breathing, in and out, over and over.

"I'm always here," Margery said in a sleepy voice. "We have a girl that comes in to clean on Mondays, and she brings the shopping. Mother doesn't want me to wander. Not here. It isn't like New York, she says."

"I would think it's safer," Sophie whispered, but fell silent when Brianna opened one eye to glare at her.

Then Margery gasped.

"What is it, Margery?" Brianna asked calmly.

"Ten… no, eleven days ago, I went to a party," she said. "I didn't stay long. I didn't really know anyone. It was strange. I only went because my mother wanted me to."

"She wanted you to go out?" Brianna asked.

"Wanted? Kind of. She didn't insist, but I could tell that she really wanted me to go. I had lots of friends back in New York. I don't really have any friends here. But it was weird. It was the daughter of one of her clients, and all the girls at the party knew that's why I was invited."

I bit my lip. That sounded like a truly dismal way for poor Margery to spend an afternoon.

"So someone might have taken your pin out of its box while you were at this party?" Brianna asked.

"But no one knew it was there," Margery insisted, and she was losing the calm she had gained from the breathing.

Brianna noticed this even before I did, taking long slow breaths herself until Margery was lulled back into matching her.

"There was something else you noticed," Sophie said. I glanced back at her. She was sitting on the edge of the bed with her eyes half-closed. She didn't seem to be so much looking at Margery as looking all around Margery. Sensing something, I guessed. "Did you know the hatpin was gone?"

"No," Margery said in her sleepy voice. "I didn't check. I don't open it much. What if I got caught?"

"But something happened," Brianna prompted.

"That night," Margery said. "I woke up thirsty. I went down to get a glass of water. While I was downstairs, I heard my mother moving around upstairs. It was two or three hours after midnight, about the time she finishes work for the night, so it wasn't strange that she was awake. And when I went back upstairs, she was in her own room again. I don't know what that means."

Then her eyes flew open, and she looked at each of us in turn. "You don't think my mother killed your friend? She's a cheat and a fraud and sometimes a thief, but never a killer."

"We don't think that," I insisted, earning me a warning look from the other two, but I didn't care. I didn't think Cora had done it.

"How do you know this is the thing they used to kill her?" Margery asked. "That might not be blood."

"I'm sorry, Margery, but we really are sure about that," Brianna said.

"We don't think Cora did this," I said. "Do we?"

"All signs are pointing this way," Sophie said. "I mean, come on. It's her or Margery, and we really don't think it's Margery."

"Maybe she just handed the hatpin to someone else who used it to murder Mrs. Olson, then Cora put the pin back again," I said.

"Brianna, explain Occam's razor to her," Sophie said, and Brianna actually opened her mouth before I threw up my hands to thwart her.

"Never mind!" I said.

"That little light," Margery said, looking inside the battered old box at her other little treasures. "That silver light. You made that happen." She looked up at Brianna.

"It led me to your hatpin," Brianna said, taking the vial of Mrs. Olson's blood and tears out of her pocket to show Margery. "Because it's the same blood as from our friend."

"That's real magic," Margery said.

"Yes," Brianna agreed.

Margery's hands twisted in her lap until she clasped them together and forced them to be still.

"Can you commune with spirits? I mean, for real?"

"No one can do that," Brianna said, then reached out to put her own hand over both of Margery's. "I'm sorry. Some secrets aren't ours to know."

"But Miss Zenobia..." I said, the words out of my mouth before I could stop them.

"Was a very powerful witch, who gave up years of her life to project an aspect of herself across time," Brianna said, giving Margery's hands a squeeze. "We didn't summon her. We only spoke to a piece of herself that she had willfully, and at great cost, left behind."

"Like a ghost?" Margery asked.

"Different," Brianna said.

"It's a mind bend, kid," Sophie said. "I still don't understand it all."

"But I've heard spirits," Margery said.

"I thought you knew everything your mother did was all tricks?" Brianna said with a frown.

"I don't mean that," Margery said. "I know how she projects her voice and does accents and everything. That's not what I'm talking about. The spirit I've heard doesn't talk to her, I don't think. It only talks to me." She slumped down over the hands folded in her lap again, not wanting to look any of us in the eye. "I don't like it. It's a voice in my head. I don't think it's human. I don't think it ever was human."

"Not from a deceased person, you mean?" I asked.

"I don't know what it is. It's inside my mother's crystal ball."

Brianna sighed and sat back on her heels. "Sophie and I looked over all of those things carefully, before, during and after your mother's show. I promise you there's nothing magical about any of them. It's all tricks."

"Not that one," Margery said. "The other one. The one she's had the longest but never uses."

"Where is it?" I asked.

Margery bit her lip and clenched her hands, but quickly decided she had to show us. Brianna followed her back out of the room. Sophie nudged me with her elbow and held her beaded bag open until I slipped the hatpin inside. It didn't quite fit, but it was more convenient than stretching out my sweater sleeve to hold it in my hand.

Margery had taken Brianna into the parlor, and they were crouched in front of the cabinet under the window, the cabinet I had recognized from Mina's house. Margery opened a chipped little black lacquer box with an ornate lotus on the cover and took out a little key which she fitted into the lock, turning it with a click.

I couldn't see what was inside that square space, but I felt like all the hair on the back of my neck was standing up in a bristling wave. Like the air was full of static electricity. Potential energy waiting for a spark.

Margery sat back on her heels, a bundle wrapped in faded velvet in her hands. She carefully peeled back the edges, not touching the object hidden within.

There was no burst of light, no sun-dappled patterns or flares of silver power. But the moment the dull, imperfectly round sphere lay exposed on Margery's velvet-covered palms, Sophie and Brianna both gasped and recoiled.

I don't know what they saw. I didn't see anything myself. But the moment my eyes rested on the dark, mottled thing, I felt a stab of agonizing hot pain like a lance through my gut.

I also vaguely felt the floor when it rushed up to meet me, but mostly it was my belly on fire that consumed me. I wrapped my arms around my middle and begged all the powers in the universe for the pain to pass.

It only stabbed me harder.

CHAPTER 17

*A*nd then, as suddenly as it started, it stopped.

I lifted my head and saw Margery clutching the now-covered crystal ball in both hands as if it might be about to jump away from her.

"That was..." Sophie started, but words failed her.

"What was that?" Brianna asked. "I've never felt anything like it. It was immense, smothering, but... alive?"

"Alive," Sophie agreed. "Definitely alive."

"And magic?" I asked from where I was pushing myself up off the floor.

"Definitely magic," Sophie said. "Are you all right?"

I nodded. I was still breathing in little halting gasps, viscerally afraid that the pain was going to come back, but it didn't seem to be.

"I think it hates you," Margery said, blinking back tears. "I felt it. It really hates you."

I couldn't argue with that assessment.

"It was speaking to you just now?" Brianna asked. Margery nodded, head bowed low. "What did it say?"

"I can't repeat it," Margery said, shaking her head emphatically.

"Foul language?" Brianna asked.

"No," Margery said. "I mean, yes, but that's not why. I can't say it out loud. When you say things out loud, sometimes they happen."

"What kind of things?" Brianna asked.

"No, I won't say," Margery said firmly, then thrust the ball in its velvet coverings into Brianna's hands. She hadn't wrapped it particularly neatly, and Brianna fumbled to keep from touching the glass as she took it. Margery got to her feet and ran out of the room, but stopped to linger in the foyer, uncertain.

"Is the power inside of that thing somehow involved in Mrs. Olson's murder?" I asked.

"I guess there's only one way to find out," Brianna said, swallowing hard. Then she got up and carried the ball over to the little table in the center of the room, pushing Cora's other crystal ball aside to set the real one down.

"What one way?" I asked, climbing into the nearest of the chairs. "What are you going to do?"

"Look at it, I guess," Brianna said, glancing up at Sophie. "Ask it some questions. Right?" Sophie gave a hesitant nod.

Brianna clutched the edge of the velvet between two fingertips, but stopped to look up at me.

"Are you sure you want to be here?" she asked. "You seem sensitive to this thing's power."

"It's not a sensitivity, I don't think," Sophie said, her eyes unfocused as she looked around me rather than at me. "No, I agree with Margery. The ball attacked her specifically. I wonder why?"

"Maybe you should go stand by Margery?" Brianna suggested.

"No," I said, sitting up straighter. "I'm prepared this time. I can handle it."

"You're sure?" Brianna asked.

No. No, I wasn't.

"I'm sure," I said.

Brianna pulled the cover away with the flourish of a magician pulling a tablecloth out from under a place setting. She half raised a hand as if to shield her eyes from a glare, and Sophie had both of her hands up as if about to begin one of her dances.

But nothing happened. The crystal ball just sat in its nest of faded velvet.

Waiting, I thought. But for what?

"What's it doing?" Brianna whispered, looking up at Sophie.

"I'm not sure," Sophie whispered back.

"Do you hear that?" I asked, although I don't think what I was sensing was so much a sound as a vibration. Low but constant, making my heart flutter as it echoed through my chest.

Margery, hovering near the doorway, clutching one of the French doors, whimpered.

"I see it," Sophie said. "It's sort of filling the room around us. Like wisps of power dancing around the chairs."

Brianna looked around, eyes wide, but I didn't see anything at all. I watched as she and Sophie followed the motion of various things with their eyes, but all I felt was the same constant humming, never louder or stronger, but never fading.

"Maybe I should try speaking to it," Brianna said, leaning closer to the crystal ball. She slid into Cora's own chair and moved her hands around the sphere of glass, never quite touching it.

"No change," Sophie said, still watching invisible things dance around us.

"Spirit of the crystal, will you not speak with us?" Brianna asked. Her hands stretched, fingers splayed wide.

"Don't touch it," I said as her middle fingers strayed closer to the dark glass.

"Maybe I should try something with the dancing wisps," Sophie suggested, raising her arms and swinging them to one side as if to start a spin.

That little motion was all it took. The low hum became a deep rhythmic boom, like a giant in heavy boots drawing ever nearer, making the walls, the very ground beneath us, shake.

I heard Margery scream, then the crash as she flung open the front door and fled the house. Then the booms were too loud to hear anything else. I pressed my hands over my ears and looked up at Sophie desperately.

Sophie had staggered back, her dance move never even truly begun. She threw her arms around her head as if to protect her face from attack, but just as one of her heels crossed the line from parlor to foyer, she pulled herself together, drawing up straight and spreading her arms wide, then gathering them close. Then she was spinning and dancing, but it did no good. The earth beneath us quaked so hard I expected the house to collapse and crush us at any moment.

I heard another sound, all but lost amidst the booming, but definitely there. A woman was screaming and laughing, both at once.

I got to my feet. I'm not sure if I intended to make a run for the door or to try to smash the brightly glowing ball on the center of the table, but I was incapable of trying either. The ground bucked beneath me and spilled me backwards, tossing me over the back of my chair to land against the cabinet. The edge drove into the side of my lower back, just below my ribs, and knocked the wind out of me.

I fell to the ground, clutching the soft carpeting as if it could anchor me. I felt something under my palm, a tiny rounded shape of cold metal.

"What have you done?!?" Cora screeched at us, and I lifted my head to see her standing framed by the French doors, her hair whipping around her face as if moved by an invisible wind. I had the sudden urge to laugh. Even in the midst of all of this chaos, she still found her dramatic entrance.

"This power is beyond you!" Brianna said. "What can you be thinking, meddling with such things?"

"You dare ask that of me! Interlopers! You have no right!" Cora seethed, taking a few stumbling steps across the quaking floor until she caught up against the edge of the table. She reached for the brightly glowing ball, but Brianna drew her wand.

"Do not touch that!" Brianna shouted.

"It's mine, not yours!" Cora said, but the sight of the wand now pointed at her seemed to unnerve her a bit.

"I can't control this!" Sophie cried, having been tumbled into the far corner by the bucking ground.

"Make it stop," Brianna said to Cora, still pointing her wand at her.

"Can't you?" Cora shot back, the corner of her mouth turning up in a mocking smile. Brianna looked down at the ball then changed the aim of her wand from Cora to the ball.

And just like that, I was back on the floor, writhing in pain as hot pokers stirred my insides into a slurry. My voice blended with the laughing/screaming woman's.

Then something else slammed. The front door again. I heard male voices now. Edward and Otto. Someone was trying to touch me, but I couldn't bear it. Anything on my skin was like a cattle brand of searing hot metal. I shrieked and squirmed away.

"No!" I heard Sophie yell in her most commanding voice, but her tone of command ended in an undignified squeal that dopplered away from me.

Then, suddenly, everything was still. No screams of laughter, no pounding of approaching doom, no quaking floor.

No pain.

I sat up, pushing the sweaty mass of my hair out of my eyes. I pulled myself up using the cabinet for support. The blackout curtains had fallen to the ground, and I saw Sophie out on the front walk, trying to break free of Otto's grip.

She had set it all off when she had tried to interact with it. Now that she was out of the house, it was all done.

At least for now.

"Are you all right?" Edward asked, his hands reaching out but not touching me, as if afraid a touch might hurt me.

A minute ago, it had.

"Yes, I'm fine," I said. I felt like I'd run a double marathon then got hit by a truck, but compared to a minute ago, anything was fine. I wanted to summon a reassuring smile for him to back up my words, but I just couldn't. There was a feeling of something bad about to happen, like one of us was about to say or do something that would start the whole nightmare up again.

"You get out of my house," Cora seethed at us. "All of you. Out."

Somewhere I couldn't see, Margery was snuffling.

Leaning on Edward's arm more than I would want to admit, I started to make my way to the door. Sophie had finally wrenched herself free from Otto's grasp, giving him a hard shove for good measure, but she made no move to come back inside.

I don't think any of us knew what would happen if she did.

Brianna put her wand away, then reached for the edges of the velvet cover, flipping the corners up until the glass was out of sight. But when she started to gather it up, Cora's hand closed on her wrist.

"You're not taking that," she said.

"I can't let you keep it," Brianna said. "You don't even understand what you have here, do you?"

"You don't understand it either," Cora spat back.

Brianna flinched as if the words wounded her. "Not yet, but I will!" she said, rallying.

"You take one thing out of this house, and I'll call the cops," Cora warned.

It took all of my willpower not to look towards Sophie, standing outside with her beaded bag over her arm, the end of the hatpin poking out of the top.

"You're not going to call the cops," Otto said, adjusting his hat to a more menacing angle as he stepped towards the door.

"What are you doing here?" Cora asked, then started to put it all together. "Did you bring these witches to my house? Why would you do that?"

"You best be careful, Miss Fox," Otto said, his voice a low growl. "Mind what you say to me."

"Or what? You'll alter the terms of our business arrangement?" Cora asked in a mocking tone.

Otto came all the way into the house, stepping around the chaos of furniture thrown about the parlor, stopping only when he was mere inches away from Cora. She was taller than him. I mean, conceptually, I knew she had a good four inches on him. But when he leaned in to whisper at her, it felt like he loomed over her.

"Yes."

It was all he said. But Cora said nothing in response. She took half a step back, clutching the edges of her shawl over her heart and looking, frankly, just the tiniest bit frightened.

Which she never had when everything had gone insane for a minute inside her own parlor.

"Leave it," Otto said. He wasn't even looking at Brianna, but somehow he had known she was reaching for the ball again.

"Best to leave it," I said, only mouthing the words "for now." Brianna gave me a nod and came over to take my other arm and help me outside.

With the curtains down, I had gotten my wish of letting sunlight and air into the parlor, but it didn't penetrate the fog in my brain, the overwhelming sense of doom that had been pounded into me by each of those thumping footsteps. Something had been approaching, but I had never seen what. The idea that someday I might, that it was just a matter of time, hung over me like an oppressive gray blanket, muffling my very mind.

But the minute I stepped outside I smelled the aroma of dry autumn leaves carried on the breeze, felt its warmth on my skin, then the more intense heat from the sun, and that muffling blanket was gone. That feeling of crushing doom was gone.

I hadn't realized how smothered I had been feeling. To suddenly feel free again was overwhelming. I took one more step out into the sunlight. Then the world flared up at me, so bright and fresh and clean and lovely. I just couldn't take it all in. It was too much.

I closed my eyes against it, retreated within myself, and let Brianna and Edward guide me back to the car.

CHAPTER 18

J was aware of people around me, especially Edward, once more pressed close to my side as we crowded together in the front seat. I heard murmurs of voices: Sophie's voice crackling with angry energy, Brianna sounding more dejected, the faintest of German accent in Otto's words. Sometimes the murmur was my own voice answering some inquiry my brain didn't really bother processing.

I smelled the leaves on the air and the exhaust from the cars around us. The leathery new car smell.

Eventually, we stopped somewhere, another lurch as the boy pulled the parking brake before the car had quite stopped rolling. I walked up the front path mostly under my own power, Edward's arm more just to guide me as I paid no attention at all to where I was going. I just kept putting one foot in front of the other until at last I was seated on the sofa in the parlor.

I let the sounds of everyone's voices around me just wash over me, not really listening. I felt the cushion next to me sink as someone sat down on it, draping an arm over the back of the sofa behind me as they pressed something into my hands. I felt metal in the distinctive hand-friendly design of a flask and took a sip.

Suddenly, my mind was clear.

"Ooh, that's good," I said, taking another sip.

"Tea would probably be better," Sophie said sternly, taking the flask out of my hands and giving it back to Otto, who was the person who had sat down next to me.

"Better?" he asked me as he took a sip of his own, then screwed the cap back onto the flask.

"Yes, thanks," I said. "I was… I don't know."

"In shock, I think," Otto said, but there was something else in his eyes as he looked at me. Like he wanted to say more. I glanced up to see if it was Edward that was making him reticent when I spotted Coco lingering in the doorway.

"Hello, Coco," I said.

"Hello," she said. "What's going on? You guys look like you were in an armed robbery." Her face lit up at the thought. "Were you guys in an armed robbery?"

"No," I said.

"Coco, why don't you help me make some tea for everyone?" Edward said, catching the girl's shoulder and steering her out of the room.

I looked up at the others. Otto looked as cool as ever. The hat pushed back on his head had tousled his hair a bit, but that just made him look more rakish than usual.

The silk of Sophie's red dress was definitely rumpled, stained with sweat, and still sticking to her in places. The flower on the side of her hat had gotten crushed at some point.

Brianna had torn the hem of her dress, a raggedy strip of it hanging down to her ankle on one side, and her long hair was tangled and wind-blown.

Then I looked down at myself and realized, to my horror, that my sweater was dotted all over with something thick and dark. I put my hands to my face and felt a crust of dried blood under my nose.

"When did that happen?" I asked, looking up at the others in horror.

"Both times the..." Brianna glanced Otto, and her words faltered. "Both times you fell."

I knew what she meant. When the crystal ball had attacked me, when the hot pokers had jabbed all over my insides. Apparently, I had bled from my nose as well and never realized.

The Sophie touched her earlobe, and I touched my own. Both were crusty with dried blood. I was pretty sure it was also in my hair.

"We got in over our heads," I said.

"Yes, I do believe we did," Sophie said. Brianna said nothing, just looked dejected.

"I think you girls are being too hard on yourselves," Otto said.

"What would you know about it?" Sophie asked.

"More than you seem to think," Otto said. Beside me on the couch, he leaned forward with his elbows on his knees, and Brianna and Sophie took a couple of steps closer, and when he spoke again, his voice was a low rumble. "I already told you the students of this school command respect from the folks in my part of the world. You didn't really think I meant it was because you were students at a charm school, did you? I know what the Exceptional Young Ladies part means, and I know that for the three of you, it very much applies."

"What does it mean?" Sophie asked, challenge in her voice.

"Just what Cora called you," he said, then sat back and took the flask back out of his vest pocket to take another sip.

"Oh," Brianna said, blinking. "She did call us witches, didn't she?"

"She did," Sophie said, then turned her attention to Otto. "I thought you'd take that as just a slur."

"But that's not how she meant it," Otto said, offering her the flask.

"No, that's not," Sophie agreed and took a long pull from the flask.

"There were sandwiches in the icebox," Coco announced as she marched into the room with an overloaded tray of plates and the aforementioned sandwiches. She set it on the table and ran back to the kitchen for something else.

"Lovely," I said. "I should wash up before I eat, though." I started to get up, but there was one last thing niggling in my mind. I leaned in close to Otto. "Does Edward know?"

"Rumors, maybe," he said close to my ear. "He left the street life too young, I think, to have gotten to the truth and story sorting out phase. But after what he saw today, who knows what he thinks? You want me to ask him?"

"No," I said, and got up from the sofa. "If he isn't suspicious now, it's probably better if we don't make him so."

"Suit yourself," Otto said with a shrug.

"Was she swearing you to secrecy?" Sophie asked him as I headed up the stairs to the washroom. "Because you have to swear to keep our secrets."

I smiled to myself, fully confident that Otto would never leave that parlor until he had promised Sophie everything she asked for.

I made a few dabs at my face with a wet washcloth but quickly decided that was an exercise in futility and turned on the taps in the tub, sticking my entire head under the water and just letting it run over me. My ears were particularly bad; more was congealed in my ear canals than had leaked out. It was little wonder that for a while there all the sounds in the world had gotten so muted.

I wrapped my hair in a towel then went up to the attic, hoping against hope that there would be something I could wear in place of the sweater in the closets.

In the present, there were closets for each of us full of clothes that were just our size. But while the closets already existed in 1927, our clothes didn't. Instead, the closets were storing a variety of theatrical costumes entirely inappropriate for my needs. At last, stuffed in the back corner of one, I found a wadded bit of cotton that turned out to be a Yankees baseball jersey.

Strange as it might seem after the day I had just had, I felt a legitimate thrill as I realized what I was holding in my hands. A real vintage baseball jersey. It was awesome. Would anyone miss it if I took it back to 2018 and just kept it?

"Amanda?" Edward called. It sounded like he was on the first floor, but then I heard the creak of the stairs under his feet. I pulled the towel off my head and yanked on the jersey before he could catch me in my undergarments.

"Coming!" I called back down as I raced down the steps.

"Otto and I have to go," he was saying as I rounded the last landing and he could see me. He seemed to lose his train of thought for a moment. "You look better."

"I feel better," I said, stopping when I was a step above where he stood. I kind of liked how he still had to look up at me.

"That's good. Brianna kept insisting you didn't need a doctor, but..."

"You can always trust Brianna," I said. "Always."

"I'll remember that," he said, then cleared his throat before looking up at me again out of the sides of his eyes. "I don't know quite what happened today."

"Me neither," I said. "We're going to try to figure it out, though."

"And then what?" he asked.

"Then we'll do whatever is needful," I said.

He gave me a long assessing look, and I braced myself for a barrage of pointed questions, but in the end, he just shrugged. "I bet you will."

"The three of us," I said.

"Yes," he agreed. I couldn't see the front door from where I was standing, but I heard Otto in the vicinity of it clear his throat expectantly. Edward took a step backwards and started to turn to leave, but then stopped and looked back up at me.

"You're not here to learn social graces, are you?" he asked.

"Aren't I?" I countered.

"Because that's the usual business of charm schools."

"Is it?" I asked.

He gave a little laugh and made another abbreviated motion towards leaving. This time when he turned back, it was to say, "I like your jersey."

Then he was gone.

The little bubble of happiness that had been growing since I found the jersey popped the minute I was back in the parlor. Brianna was pacing a space much too small for such things. Sophie was sitting in a chair, but her bouncing foot betrayed her own agitation.

"What are we thinking?" I asked.

"We have to take that crystal ball," Brianna said. "That has far too much power to be in the hands of a charlatan."

"A charlatan who keeps it locked in a cabinet and refuses to touch it," Sophie said.

"We can't leave it so close to Margery," Brianna said. "It's dangerous."

"Margery understands that," Sophie said. "She's already protecting herself. Better than we did, actually."

"You don't think we should take it?" I surmised.

"No," Sophie said.

"Why?" I asked, surprised.

"It's not what we do," Sophie said.

"You don't think it's related to the murder?"

"No," Sophie said. "We have the murder weapon in my bag. We can find a way to get that to the police forensics team. Say we found it in the yard or something. They can take it from there."

"But what if the killer is also from 1927?" I asked.

"Let's see what the police come up with first," Sophie said.

"Whatever is inside that crystal ball, it's trying to exert an influence over others," Brianna said.

"Maybe so, but dealing with that is not our calling. Maintaining the time portal is," Sophie said.

"You're just afraid if we go back, you might get hurt," Brianna said.

"Yes," Sophie readily agreed. "I might, or you might, or Amanda. Or one of us might get killed, or trapped somehow, or any of a thousand things. We just can't risk it. We need all three of us working together to maintain the time portal. That's our job. That's our responsibility."

"Whose responsibility is that artifact being on the loose?" Brianna demanded.

"I don't know," Sophie admitted. "It seems like something someone ought to know. Isn't there a witches' council or something we can consult?"

"No," Brianna said, but then stopped to think. "I mean, not officially. We don't organize like that. But I can ask around."

"Maybe there's a book in the library that says something about that crystal ball," I said. "If it really is some sort of important artifact."

"Yes," Sophie agreed. "If we really have to fight it again, I want to know everything we can discover about it first."

"All right," Brianna agreed. "For now, we just go back home."

We went back to our own, much colder time, hustling back into the house before heading our separate ways. Brianna needed the library, of course. Sophie wanted a shower. I just desperately needed to rest my aching body.

Only when my bedroom door had closed with a resounding click did I reach my hand into the pocket of my skirt and pull out the little twist of metal I had picked up from the parlor floor of Cora's house.

The key to the cabinet. Somehow Margery had dropped it, or it had slipped from her pocket in all the chaos. And I had found it under my hand, and despite the pain I had been writhing in, I had held onto it. I had clutched it like a talisman and not let it go.

And the creepy part was, I didn't even really know why. I just had.

I set it on my nightstand, then stripped out of my 1927 clothing, stuffing them into the appropriate hamper so that they could be washed with period-correct detergents, then put back away in my closet until next time.

But the jersey I kept, wearing it as a nightshirt. So far, being a witch and guarding a time portal was a lot of intense work. A jersey wasn't much of a reward in exchange for all that, but just then, it was enough.

CHAPTER 19

woke up at five on the dot and sat up in my bed.

I had to go to Mina Fox's house. Had to.

I got up and glanced out the window as I got dressed. Overcast again and threatening rain, or maybe even sleet. Such a contrast from the day before in 1927. I pulled on jeans and a turtleneck, then a hoodie and a polar fleece vest with a waterproof hood. I started to reach for my Converse sneakers, but halfway there my hand just veered the other way and grabbed my boots.

I had experienced this feeling before, this compulsion to do or not do a thing. I had had it for years when I had stayed in my hometown after high school. Mostly it had been of shorter durations, a need to leave early for work one day or not go to school on another, and once the decision was made, the feeling went away.

I didn't expect this feeling would last any longer than it took for me to get to Mina's house, but it was coming with a lot of very specific ancillary instructions that I was just following. It was intense, almost frightening.

As this feeling directed me across the room to pick up the key I had set on my nightstand the night before and stuff it in my pocket, I reminded myself that nothing bad had ever happened because of this feeling. Quite the opposite. I didn't like being led around by the nose —who would?—but I was sure I wasn't in any danger.

I started towards the library to find Brianna and tell her where I was going, but my feet kept going past the second-floor landing. Okay, so mine was a secret mission. Again that little feeling of unease, but again I reminded myself this compulsive feeling had always looked out for me before. There must be a good reason for it.

I thought I knew that reason when I reached the bottom of the stairs and found Brianna about to head back upstairs with a cup of tea and a plate heaping with buttered toast. Of course, I shouldn't go to the library first, not if I was meant to run into Brianna on the stairs.

"Oh," Brianna said when she saw me there. "It's awfully early."

"I'm guessing for you it's very late," I said, using the moment of stillness to zip up my jacket, then my vest.

"Yeah," Brianna said, then at the sound of the zipper, really looked at me for the first time. "You're going out?"

"Just for a bit," I said. "Said" in the sense that the words came out of my mouth; my brain wasn't the one choosing them.

"Where are you going at this hour?" she asked.

"I'm hoping to catch Nick before he heads off to class," I lied easily.

"Sophie still has the hatpin," Brianna said. "We aren't ready to call the police yet."

"No, it's not about that," I said, kind of marveling at the words just spilling out of my own mouth. What a strange feeling, to hear myself speak without knowing what I was going to say next. "It's about a different thing."

Brianna opened her mouth to speak but was swept up in a massive yawn, the kind that could pop your eardrums.

"You should really get some sleep," I said.

"I will," she promised. "I just have to finish something up."

"Naps are good," I said.

"I will," she said. "I just need an hour or so."

"Okay," I said, then found myself adding, "but I'll be checking up on you. You better be napping when I get back."

Brianna yawned again, too prolonged to get words out. But she did give me a nod before heading up the stairs with her tea and toast.

I pulled up both my hoods as I stepped outside, then found gloves buried deep in the vest pockets. I was going to need them, nippy as the air was.

I was mildly surprised to find I didn't stop at the condo where Nick was living. Not even for a moment to see if his car was there or not. I just kept right on walking, nearly all the way down Summit Avenue. It took more than an hour before I was standing on Mina Fox's front porch.

Which still made it not even seven in the morning yet, but when I knocked briskly on the door, it opened almost at once.

"Good morning!" Mina said. She was wearing a fluffy robe over pajamas and was rubbing tiredly at the side of her face, but her eyes were alert, and her hair was far too neatly combed for her to have just hopped out of bed.

"Hi. Do you remember me? Amanda Clarke?" I asked.

"You're one of the nice young ladies living next door to Linda Olson," she said. "Please come in. Would you like some coffee?"

"Coffee would be great," I said and stepped into her living room.

The cabinet was right there, just as I remembered it. But Mina was smiling back at me as she headed towards the light from the kitchen, so I followed her.

I would find an opportunity, I promised myself, squeezing the key in my pocket.

"Cream? Sugar?" she asked as she took a mug out of the cupboard.

"Black is fine," I said, sitting down at the old school dining room table, the kind with drop leaves and a marble-patterned linoleum top. One of the leaves was up; the one tucked against the wall under the window was down. Two chairs were arranged on either side, and I sat down in the one facing the appliances. It did indeed look like I'd caught Mina already up and about her day, a newspaper sitting next to a half-filled cup of coffee.

She set my coffee in front of me and then topped off her own before shuffling back into the kitchen.

"Sorry to come so early," I said. I still had that weird thing of hearing myself speak the words the compulsion wanted me to say.

"Don't worry about it," Mina said with a wave of her hand. "At my age, I don't sleep much anymore. I've been up for hours."

I took a sip of my coffee. It was bitter with a taste like almonds, but it was strong. The caffeine surged straight to my brain and to my surprise that compulsive feeling started to loosen up.

Well, I had been supposed to go to Mina's house, and now here I was, so that made sense. But now that I had control over my own mouth, I didn't know what to say.

I had no idea why I was here, beyond wanting to see if that crystal ball was still in the cabinet. It seemed easier to take it from Mina, who had no idea what it was, than from Cora. And then I could bring it to Brianna.

"I'm glad that you came. I wanted to ask your advice," Mina said, setting the paper aside and setting a stack of brochures in front of me. "The matter of the will isn't quite settled yet, but they've given me some numbers, and oh my, they're overwhelming."

"What are all these?" I asked, leafing through the brochures. Food banks, clothes drives, sponsoring kids in other parts of the world. "Charities?"

"Exactly," Mina said, sipping her coffee with a smile. "I don't need a cent of that money myself. I plan to donate the house to the historical society, but I'd like to use the money for a cause that Linda Olson would have liked. But I never knew her. Do you have any idea?"

"I really didn't know her very well," I said, taking another drink of that strange coffee. Perhaps her machine needed service or at least a good cleaning. Or perhaps she was still using coffee she got a decade ago at a huge discount from one of those wholesale stores that sold things by the ton.

"I suppose I could just give it all to the historical society," Mina mused, looking out the window at the slowly brightening sky.

"You know, she might actually have liked that," I said. "She was always very interested in the neighborhood."

"Oh!" Mina cried, jumping to her feet. "I have another thought.

Something that was sent to me in the mail, but I held onto it. Let me go have a look. You'll be all right here?"

"Perfect," I said, taking another swallow of coffee.

The minute she had shuffled out of the kitchen, I leaned forward to see which way she went. I don't know if I hoped she would save me the trouble and open that cabinet herself, but in the end, she went the other way, towards her bedroom.

"It was only a week or two ago, I'm sure I still have it," Mina called, yelling over the sound of drawers sliding open and the contents being stirred about.

I set down my coffee and crept to the kitchen doorway, running one hand along the wall, then grasping the doorframe as I leaned out. No sign of Mina.

I rushed into the living room, then stopped as a wave of dizziness rushed through my brain. Too much caffeine, not enough food. Or rather, no food at all. No supper the night before. I hadn't even had any of the sandwiches Coco had brought us.

My blood sugar had to be in the single digits.

But there was nothing to do but press on and finish what I had come here to do. There were a million places I could stop for food between Mina's house and the school. I'd be fine.

I took a step, then flinched at the sound of my foot hitting the floor with approximately the gravity of Frankenstein's monster. I regretted choosing clunky boots over sneakier footwear. But the carpet was thick enough to mask the sound if I walked lightly enough.

I crossed the living room to the cabinet, then dropped down to one knee. The dizziness had lessened but not quite gone away. I could still hear Mina prattling away as she upended drawer after drawer in search of I didn't know what.

I pulled the key out of my pocket and slid it into the lock. It fit. I hadn't quite realized that I had been worried the lock would have been changed in the intervening decades.

Holding my breath, I turned the key. It slid easily, as if the lock had been recently oiled. Then I heard a click.

The space that had been crowded with dusty objects when

Margery had opened it before contained only one item now. But I recognized that faded velvet wrapped around it, as well as its palm-sized spherical shape.

"I think this is it," Mina said, and her voice was drawing closer. I reached in to seize the ball. Another wave of dizziness rolled over me, blacking out the sides of my vision, and when it passed, I realized I wasn't holding the ball, only the scrap of velvet meant to be wrapping it. Hiding it from view.

I gave my head a shake to clear it, then peered inside the cabinet. The ball was resting there. It flared brightly as if in greeting, then went dark as fast as if someone had thrown a switch the very moment Mina stepped back into the room.

"Oh," Mina said, startled to find me clearly snooping in her things, and possibly even trying to rob her.

I tried to explain, or I guess really lie, about what I was doing, but my tongue was suddenly too thick for me to move inside my mouth.

"Oh dear," Mina said, setting aside whatever thing she had been on the hunt for. It looked like yet another brochure, glossy and colorful. The gloss caught the light from the kitchen and reflected it back to me, too bright. It stabbed at my eyes. My head instantly started aching, then the vertigo hit again, and I realized I had fallen to my hands and knees.

Bitter almonds. The coffee had tasted like bitter almonds. Oh, I had been so stupid. Cyanide, the oldest poison in the book.

I had been so stupid. And the one thing I had always counted on, that feeling that guided me through my hardest days before, had just abandoned me.

I was all alone, and I was going to die.

CHAPTER 20

$\mathcal{I}$ tried to get to the front door. I really did. But somehow holding onto the back of the sofa to pull myself up became slumping into the sofa and then gravity was just too strong for me to get up again.

"You know, I was so worried you wouldn't even drink the coffee," Mina said as she walked past me to the cabinet. I was slumped too low on the sofa to turn my head and see what she was doing. But she kept on talking. "I was sure you would be too suspicious of me. But I thought maybe you'd take a sip, just to be polite. So to be on the safe side, I really dosed it. I had to make that one sip count."

I heard a grunt as she straightened up from a crouch and then she was back in my line of sight, holding the naked crystal ball in one hand so casually I knew she didn't truly understand its power.

She leaned in, a triumphant smile in her eyes. "But you just drank it all down, didn't you? That is a touch inconvenient. I had hoped to have sent you on your way before you keeled over. You dying in my living room isn't exactly ideal, but I'm sure we'll manage." She turned her attention to the ball in her hand. "Won't we?"

I closed my eyes, focusing on my breathing. It kept wanting to just stop. My lungs didn't seem to be working as a team so well anymore, and everything hurt, and I was so tired.

I felt Mina leaning in closer and opened my eyes, or tried to. I managed to get one to squint up about halfway.

"Still with us?" she said. I tried to give her a death glare, but I doubt I projected much. And even that took too much attention away from focusing on keeping my lungs going. A black tunnel was starting to close around the edges of my vision.

"You know what this is, don't you?" Mina asked, holding the ball between us, so close I could snatch it from her if I could still move my arms. "You must know if you came here to take it from me. Do you?"

I watched her out of that half an eye but kept focusing on my breath. She waited expectantly for an answer for far too long before giving up with a shrug.

"You must know. It's power," she said, holding the ball up in the air. "Great power that could have changed everything for my family if only my mother hadn't been so closed off to it. If only my grandmother hadn't been so afraid of it. But I'm open-minded, and I'm not afraid. And soon I'll have everything."

She glanced over at me as if I had said something and a look of annoyance crossed her face.

"No, it's not about the money," she said. "I already told you, I'm as well off as I could ever hope to be. Why does everyone always think everything is about the money? No, this is about revenge. Revenge on the family that destroyed mine. Revenge generations in the making, but finally ours."

My eye was starting to slip closed.

"Hey, stay awake!" Mina shouted, suddenly close to my face. Paralyzed as most of my body was, I still flinched away from her. Given the little grin that played across her lips, she found that reaction very gratifying.

"The spirit in the ball helped me to get my family's revenge, but now it's my turn to help it in its quest. And do you know what it wants more than anything? It wants the Witches Three. That's what it calls you. It's been waiting so long for you. And here you come, throwing yourself right into my lap. How delicious. One down, two to go."

This time I deliberately closed my eyes, or let that half-open eye close. Whatever. I remembered every meditation session I had done with Sophie, how she had instructed me to focus not just on my breath, but on every cell in my body. I did that now, first taking an inventory and then assessing what strength I had left.

There was a little. Not much. But maybe enough.

I lurched forward, and Mina stumbled back out of my way, but I only managed half a step before I was falling again. Mina grabbed the edge of her coffee table and pulled it out of the way before I could land on her precious tchotchkes.

I suppose I should be grateful. The padded carpet was softer than the hard edges of that table. But not by much.

"Go ahead, tire yourself out," Mina said, hovering close like a kid cheering on his turtle in a race. "Speed your way to your inevitable end. I certainly don't need you alive to lure the other two here. One by one, I will take you all down."

I ignored her. I didn't have the strength to get on my hands and knees, but I could still squirm forward on my belly like a soldier under barbed wire.

The front door was so very far away.

"I know a little about you, you know," Mina went on, bent over me so that her upside-down eyes were close to mine. "I know that the red-headed witch is the one with all the knowledge of things, but she's timid. I know the black witch has more raw power than even she knows how to access. Both together might present a challenge, but one by one they'll be no real trouble. Not for the spirit inside the crystal ball.

"But you? You, I didn't even need the ball's help for. You don't have even a hint of power, do you? And you came here all alone with not even a weapon on you. So you're not particularly bright either."

I tried to ignore her, to focus on what I was doing, but having someone else list all your faults for you out loud, to confirm your darkest fears about your own shortcomings when she's only met you once, it's hard to tune that out.

My grasping fingers couldn't clutch the carpet well enough to pull myself further ahead. I couldn't draw up a knee to advance my foot. I pressed my forehead to the floor and tried not to choke on the oily, mildewy smell of the carpet. I could scarcely breathe, and every breath was a torture.

I felt something warm against my buttock, like a rod that was heating itself up. I couldn't figure out what Mina was doing until I finally realized it wasn't her. It was my wand.

My wand was getting warmer? What did that mean?

Nothing helpful, when I lacked the strength to even reach for it, to take it out of my pocket and hold it in my hand. Even if I could manage that, what then?

Surely I was imagining the warmth.

With one last supreme effort, I rolled my head to one side, to get free of the stink from the carpet. Mina was still bent low over me, dangling her head to look me in the face. Her expression was pure delight. Watching me die was clearly making her day.

My tongue was thick in my mouth, bloated and inert like a dead fish washed up on a rocky shore. But I coaxed one last word out of my throat.

"Why?"

Mina laughed. "Why?" she repeated. "Goodness, I never even thought to ask. It was just a bargain, a promise to exchange revenges. Like strangers on a train, only one of us is, strictly speaking, not currently human. We've been planning this together since I was a small child. My mother would bring me with her to visit my grandmother, and I would always find a way to slip away, to hunt through the things my grandmother kept hidden and my mother pretended didn't exist. I admit, there were times when I thought the time for our little bargain would never come. Always I was waiting, waiting for the arrival of the ones the ball wanted me to help destroy. Waiting while the ones I wished to revenge myself upon grew fewer and fewer until they were only one. Oh, I was so afraid she'd just die, and I'd never get a chance to make anyone pay. But I did. Oh yes, I did."

My eyes were closed again, but I could still see something. A glow from the crystal ball in Mina's hand. It was glowing so brightly it penetrated my eyelids, holding back the darkness that wanted to take me.

Then I realized that the darkness was death, and the spirit inside the crystal ball wasn't going to let me die. It wanted something else for me. Something far worse than death.

My mouth was no longer capable of opening up to scream. I couldn't even warble my vocal cords. But my mind, my mind could scream and scream and scream without having to pause for breath.

And it did.

CHAPTER 21

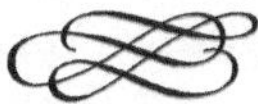

The screaming suddenly stopped, and the silence was like the coldest, purest, longest drink of water after a march across the desert in full burning sun. I drank it in, and all the pain I had been working so hard to tune out was just gone.

And I opened my eyes to find myself back in the world of silvery light. I searched for the patterns in the millions of interlocking silver strands and realized I was still in Mina's apartment, not the charm school. I could sense the outline of Mina still standing over me, dark and mundane.

But the crystal ball in her hand was something else. It glowed like a light, fiercely bright, and yet was the blackest darkness I had ever seen. It was emitting darkness in fierce beams, like the hottest sun. I stumbled back away from that darkness and tried to shield my face from it.

"Amanda," a woman's voice called.

I knew that voice. I had heard it before. Where had I heard it before?

"Who's there?" I called. The shadow of Mina seemed frozen in time, unaware of me as I got to my feet and looked around.

"Here I am," the woman said, and I turned around to find her standing behind me. For a moment, just a moment, I thought I was looking at Miss Zenobia Weekes. But this woman was different, younger. She wore her hair in an elaborate weave of braids that piled on her head only to cascade loosely around her shoulders. So very different from Miss Zenobia's severe updo, and still with a lot of black mixed in with the silvery gray. The white dress she wore was a simple sheath with a braided cord around her waist. It looked like something from the Middle Ages, where Miss Zenobia had dressed like a lady from the Civil War era when I had met her ghost.

"Who are you?" I asked. She looked younger, but dressed older. What did that mean?

"You know," the woman said with an indulgent smile.

"You're a Weekes," I said, and she nodded.

"My name is Juno," she said. "But that's not really the answer to your question, is it?"

"No," I said.

"Then look deeper. Look at me with all your senses." She smiled at me, waiting for me to figure this out. She looked like she could happily wait forever.

I could see and hear in this web world, but smell and taste didn't exist here, and touch was a very different sensation. Instead, I examined the web around her closely, following the path of each individual thread. As if indulging me, she lifted her arms, then took a few steps forward, then back again.

"You're not part of the threads," I realized. "You have your own inner structure, not connected to anything around you."

"That's more true than you know," she said with a sad smile. "Oh, Amanda. You understand so much more than you think you do."

"Why are you here?" I asked, ignoring the compliment.

"To save you," she said. "Just as I did once before."

"From Helen," I said, and she nodded. But that didn't explain why her voice was familiar. No one had spoken to me that time, although something outside of me had filled me with power. Was it just because she sounded like Miss Zenobia?

But no. Juno's soft voice was nothing like Miss Zenobia's harsh, not to be trifled with tone of command.

I turned my attention to the ball generating wave after wave of darkness. "Do you know what this is?" I asked.

"I do," she said, in a voice that told me she wouldn't explain further.

"Can I destroy it?" I asked.

"Do you want to?"

"Kind of," I admitted.

"Be careful, Amanda," she said. "In magic, you always must be very specific with your goals. You have to know exactly what outcomes you want if you're to find the best means of achieving them."

"Why does it glow darkness like that?" I asked.

"Very good question," Juno said indulgently. I suspected that, like her sister, she had been a teacher. "But let's not start there. Look at the rest of the world. What do you see?"

"Intersecting threads of light," I said.

"What you perceive as light and dark isn't really about color or light at all," she said.

"No, I thought it was about magic," I said.

"Not all magic," Juno said. "Magic is a huge, vast thing. No one can perceive all of it. Your friend Sophie sees a very specific part of magic that focuses on emotions and intent. Brianna sees the world through physics and math. But this version of the world, this is all yours. I can see it almost as you can, but not quite."

"But how can it be mine? I have no power but what you gave me. How come this isn't your version of the world, and I'm the one almost seeing it?"

"Another excellent question," Juno said. "Perceiving the world as others do is very difficult. I've had centuries of practice, and still, there are only a very few world-views close enough to mine for me to perceive them."

"But I'm young, and I don't have any power. How can I have a version of magic I can perceive?"

"You have magic," Juno said. "Just as I did. Throughout the millennia, there have been less than a handful that perceive magic the way we do. Not as light or dark, not as right or wrong, not as order or chaos. Not as a thing and its opposite all mixed up together."

"But I am seeing two things," I said. "The silver light and that black glow from the crystal ball."

"You're young yet," Juno said. "You'll learn nuance."

"But what am I seeing?" I demanded. "I thought it was the interconnectedness of all things since I see the web forming the table and sofa just as much as it forms Mina or my own body. But you aren't part of it, and neither is that ball."

"Look again," Juno said. I was getting more than a little impatient with that tone of infinite patience.

I didn't breathe in this world, so I couldn't take a deep breath first, but I did sort of gather myself together mentally. Then I looked at the threads again, at the patterns they formed as they joined and diverged. It reminded me of something, an old story.

"Is it fate or something?" I asked. "The Greek goddess who weaves the cloth? Not Arachne. The one with the spinning sister and the cutting sister."

"Lachesis," Juno said, but then pressed me again. "Is fate really the word you're looking for? Think carefully."

I looked at the patterns again. Fate wasn't the word I wanted. It implied something preordained, unchangeable. And what I saw was happening all around me, slowly and in small increments, but without a blueprint. I don't know how I knew that, I just did.

"Story," I said. "I see stories?"

"And what do you need for a story to work?" Juno asked. "The single most basic thing?"

I threw up my hands. I had no more answers.

"Time," Juno said. "Things have to happen in a sequence, or a story makes no sense."

"Time," I said. "I see time?"

Juno gave a noncommittal shrug. "You see time as you perceive it. Let's go with that for now."

"So the crystal ball is a separate thing because it has no story?"

"But you see its influence. It's glowing, isn't it?" she asked.

"So what is it?"

"It's an object of great power; you already know that. But its power has been limited, because it's been taken outside of time."

"But people can touch it and it… does stuff."

"Indeed. Imagine the destruction if it were at full power," Juno said grimly. "But as it is, its influence is severely restricted. It exists, but only across an array of fixed points. But across that array, it exists at every point simultaneously."

"Why would anyone do such a thing?" I asked.

"To contain it," Juno said. Then added, "some witches have access to power far greater than they have finesse. This isn't the last example of a brute force spell you'll encounter, I'm sure."

I tried to study the glow from the ball, but it was too hard. It felt like an abomination; it made me physically ill to look at it too long. Which was weird, since I was pretty sure in that moment I wasn't even in my physical body.

I looked down and saw a form sprawled out on the floor, the web of intersecting lines that defined it splitting away, the knots growing dimmer. No, not in my body.

I looked up at Juno again, at how the web never touched her.

"What are you?" I asked. She didn't answer, just waited with that little smile on her face. "Are you outside of time as well?"

"Am I glowing darkly?"

"No, but you're not behaving normally either."

"What do I look like to you?"

"You have the same silvery light. You're made up of a web of threads that form intersections and knots and things, just like every-thing else. But you're not connected to anything else."

"No, indeed, I have been severed from everything," she said.

"Who would do such a thing?" I asked, reviled.

"We're not ready for that discussion yet," Juno said.

"Who *could* do such a thing?" I asked as my horror deepened. This was an abomination even more vile than the crystal ball.

"Amanda, you do realize that is you down there, your body on the edge of death?" Juno said, all but snapping her fingers to redirect my attention. "Time runs differently when you're in this perceptual state, but it still runs. It will run out."

"What do I do?" I asked, hovering over my own inert form. "Can I fix myself?"

"No. But I can."

"How can you? You aren't part of the rest of the world," I said. Which brought me back around to, "what are you?"

"I'm a friend," Juno said. "I gave you power before when you needed it, and I can give it to you again now. Power enough to save yourself from the poison. Power enough to do as you will with this meddlesome woman."

"I'm not asking for revenge," I said.

"I know," Juno said. "You turned it down before, with Helen."

"Helen was misled," I said. "So was Mina, by that thing in her hand."

"I don't think you know what it means to me, that you finally came into the world and came here, to where I am. You with your ability to see not just time but story. You understand all the elements and your compassion humbles me."

I don't want to say I'm not the sort of person who can take a compliment, but I am the sort of person who's maybe too aware that most people have reasons for doing things that very seldom come down to simply being nice.

And there was something deeply suspicious of someone praising your compassion who, just the second before, had offered you bloody revenge as if it were a treat.

I was being manipulated.

"Why didn't Miss Zenobia ever tell us she had a sister?" I asked.

"She never speaks of me," Juno said.

"Why?"

"Amanda, time grows short," she said, and indeed we could both see the scant threads that remained inside my body. They were fraying, pulling away from each other. Ending my story.

"You gave me power before, without my asking for it. What's different this time?"

Juno said nothing.

"You could do it again. You don't need my consent. But I think maybe this time I could see it coming. I could stop you. I could turn down your gift."

"Don't," Juno said, her hands raised imploringly. "I need you."

"Ah," I said. "A bargain. Like the one Mina made with that... whatever is in there."

"I can save you from the poison," she said.

"At what cost?"

"I can give you so much power you can set your friends free. You'll be so powerful there won't need to be three of you serving the call. They can return to their lives, to the work and friends and family and lovers they left behind."

I tried to tune her out, to think, but I felt a stab at her words. Brianna and Sophie had given up so much to be here. I had given up nothing at all. And if my magic truly was based on time...

"Together we can do more even than that," Juno went on. "We could save your other friend as well. Linda Olson. We can change those events. If we destroy that anomaly in Mina's hand, we can change all of it."

"I don't know much about magic," I said. "But I do know something about time travel. Changing things that already happened is never a good idea."

"Anything can be changed," Juno said. "No one will remember but you and me."

"You," I said. I was so close to putting it all together. It was maddening. "You. Miss Zenobia's sister. Whom she never..."

But she had. She had mentioned a sister. Only once, and not directly. What had she said? When she was demanding that we three swore to protect the time portal, to stand guard over it.

"Time is short," I said, remembering. "That's what she said. She had made the time portal stable, but she could not collapse it. It will stand for all time, and we will guard it for what span of years is ours."

"Amanda," Juno said, pleading.

"I am a witch," I said, taking out my wand. Touch was strange here, but I still felt the warmth of its wood on my nonphysical palm.

"Amanda, please. Time..."

"Is short?" I finished, pointing the wand at her. "That's what Miss Zenobia said. Then she said—with such pain and such regret—she said, 'oh my sister.'"

"Amanda."

"She's the one that severed you from time," I said. "Isn't she?"

Juno fled.

I didn't pursue her; I just watched the wake as she moved through the world, never part of it. I saw the world as time, but not as distance. I knew the moment she returned to the school, to the backyard.

To the spot where the time portal was anchored in our time. She settled in among the binding spells and weavings that Brianna and Sophie had shored up so strongly, but they hadn't been able to see what I could see. They couldn't see Juno, and without Juno there was no portal.

I had to get home. I had so much to tell them.

CHAPTER 22

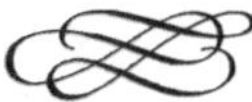

 y body didn't look good. There were still threads running through it, but one by one they were dimming. I was becoming less a part of that world.

I was suddenly certain that if I shifted my consciousness back to my physical form, I would promptly die.

I looked down at the wand in my hand. Was there something I could do to fix things?

I could feel the texture of the wood, the warmth that was more from my own hand warming it as I gripped it tight. It was the one thing I could feel in this web world.

And yet it wasn't connected to me. None of its threads interlocked with mine. It was supposed to be an extension of my own being, and yet I could see clearly that it was completely separate.

I shifted its position so that it was laying across both my palms, resting on them without me gripping it. Then I focused on its threads, but I couldn't move them. They didn't even twitch.

I briefly regretted not taking Juno's offer of power. Then I shoved that thought aside. Not helpful.

Instead, I focused on my own threads. I focused on everything that was me, that made me who I was, especially in this place that was supposed to represent my own view of magic. And then I just flowed into the wand.

The wand took my energy thirstily. Then it started pulling more and more out of me, like a vampire growing stronger as it pulled my lifeblood out of my neck. I don't know if it makes any sense to say so when I didn't actually have a head at the time, but "lightheaded" covers the feeling pretty well.

Then, just as I was too drained to remain conscious, it all started flooding back into me. All I had poured in and more, flowing through me. It coursed through every inch of my body, filling me with a sense of power.

Then, most beautiful of all feelings, it started to circulate between me and the wand I had created. The wand I had sanded and polished, the wand I had brought into being from a single branch of the tree that had sheltered my father in his last minutes.

I felt like I could see him, like I was floating over him. Then I sensed my mother as well, staggering in pain from the accident that had just happened and the birth that was only beginning.

And I sensed myself, new to the world.

Then the power settled into a rhythm between me and my wand, and the other sensations faded.

I guessed we were bonded now.

I looked down at my body and then pointed my wand at it. I didn't have any idea of what sort of spell I could cast in this place or how to do magic of any sort. I just kind of asked my wand to take care of it.

The power flowed through me, through my wand, and through my physical form. It wasn't a smooth flow. There were a lot of glitches and bottlenecks, and finally, I had to give up. It was never going to be smooth and perfect, but it was enough. I could get back into my own body without dying now.

I looked over at Mina, still standing over me with the crystal ball in her hand. Juno had said that I didn't want to destroy it, and I didn't think I *did* want to, but on the other hand, could I trust Juno?

Perhaps taking it from Mina would be enough. I reached out, but my hand couldn't grasp it. I didn't pass through it; it was more like my arm arced around it, although I was sure I was moving it in a straight line. Still, affecting it from here was going to require skills I didn't have.

I let go of my consciousness, of my awareness of the world of silvery webs.

And I opened my eyes.

Mina was still dangling over me with an air of triumph that turned to something like fright as she sprang away the moment my gaze met hers.

"How?" she demanded as I got clumsily to my feet.

"Come on now, Mina Fox," I said, pulling the wand from my back pocket. "You know I'm a witch."

Mina threw her arms up to protect her face, dropping the crystal ball as she scrambled for the cover of the sofa. I let her run. She was a secondary concern.

Still pulling my sleeve down over my hand, I bent and picked up the crystal ball. I remembered the black glow it had in my other worldview, but I didn't sense it here. It had a different feeling here, more... human?

"Mina," I said, and she gave a soft cry from behind the sofa. "Tell me true. What's in this thing? Is it a spirit or what?"

"You'll never understand it," Mina said.

"Humor me," I said. "It makes bargains and wants revenge and all sorts of human things. Is it human?"

"It is beyond anything you know," Mina snapped.

"I kind of doubt it," I said. I walked around the end of the sofa until I was standing over her, cowering on the floor. I didn't like that. It made me feel ugly. Like when an abused dog cowers away from you, a person who never ever hit dogs. Who never would.

"I'm not going to hurt you," I said.

"That's not what the spirit in the crystal says," Mina said. "You're supposed to be dead."

"Has it just been the two murders, then?" I asked. "Linda Olson, and then me?"

Mina stared at the floor sullenly.

"Why?" I asked. "I know not money, but I don't believe it was simple revenge, either. I've met your mother. How could she have raised anyone so angry as you?"

"You met my mother when she was very young," Mina sneered.

"Oh, so you know about that?" I asked.

"She changed," Mina said. "Long before I was born, she changed."

I looked at the ball in my hand. I couldn't see anything but darkness in its depths. But it had done so much evil in the world. Was I sure I didn't want to destroy it?

"I'm so sorry," I said. "I'm new at all this witch stuff. I think if we had encountered each other later in life, I might have done better."

"All you were supposed to do was die," Mina said.

"Mina," I said, dropping down on one knee but carefully holding the ball behind me, out of her reach. "This thing whispered to you. It made a bargain with you. What did it promise you? It was more than revenge."

"Power," Mina said. "Oh, why did it take so long?"

"What sort of power?" I asked. "You were already rich. Killing Linda Olson made you richer. But that's not the sort of power you mean, is it?"

"I wanted real power," Mina said. "To never again be helpless."

"To control time, maybe?" I asked.

"What?" Mina asked, and I could see that she wasn't faking surprise.

"That sort of power?" I persisted. "To move through time, go back to your own childhood or your mother's or even your grandmother's and change things?"

"Can you do that?" she asked, barely a whisper.

"No," I said, shocked. "Mina, I'm not offering you anything. I'm asking what this thing was offering you. Anything like that?"

She looked at me, genuinely puzzled. Clearly, we were speaking at cross purposes.

I sighed, then got back to my feet, taking a step away before bringing the ball back around in front of me where I could look at it again. I had wanted to be sure that it wasn't some other aspect of Juno speaking to the Fox girls through this conduit. I didn't think it was. Surely changing the timeline would have been what she offered to Mina, just as she had tried to offer it to me.

But I don't think I ruled it out. I didn't know what I was holding.

"You speak of bargains and offers and deals and what not," Mina said, pulling herself up onto her feet with the support of the back of the sofa. "You don't understand it at all. That entity inside the crystal ball isn't some separate thing from me. It's a part of me. We are as one. It gives me power. It summoned my grandfather's mother's hatpin from across time because it knew the symbolic power of using that to murder the last of that family's descendants."

"How did that happen?" I asked. "Did you go to the orchard behind the charm school?"

"No," Mina said, confused. "My mother had told me about it. Her most prized possession. And when the ball and I were planning the murder, I suggested it. I thought it was ignoring me, but when I went to the house to kill that woman, I had a gun with me. I was going to use it, inelegant as it was, but then the ball told me to look at the dressing table in the master bedroom. I crept up the stairs, and there it was, exactly as my mother had described it. The hatpin."

"Okay," I said, interrupting before Mina could tell me the gruesome details of the murder itself. I didn't need to hear them. "What did you do with it afterwards?"

"Dropped it in the yard and walked away," Mina said. "Just as the crystal ball told me to."

"And have you gotten your power?" I asked with a tired sigh. I don't think I had succeeded in removing the poison from my body. I had fought it back, a little, but the numbness was coming back. I was, once more, running out of time.

"That will grow within me once I move into the house," Mina said. "The ball and I will become as one."

I looked down at my hand. My fingers were starting to shake. Soon Mina would notice. I didn't fancy laying inert on the floor while she taunted me for a second time.

"You and the ball are as one," I said musingly.

"We always have been," Mina said. "That was how I found it. It called to me. I was barely eight, but I knew the moment I held it that it was like me. It understood me. It was like we shared a soul."

"Well," I said, looking at the ball resting on my sleeve-covered palm. "That would explain why it keeps feeling kind of familiar to me. Here."

I tossed the ball towards her. She jumped in surprise, then realized that the ball was falling towards the floor and lunged forward to catch it.

For her age, she was amazingly athletic. She straightened up; the crystal ball cuddled close to her chest like an infant. She smiled down at it with a repulsive fondness.

Somehow, my wand and I, we just knew what to do. We sensed the threads without moving to the other world and knit them together. Mina was right, they were meant for each other. Like interlocking blocks, the square peg in the square hole. Keeping them apart would have been harder than fitting them together was.

Then Mina was gone, and the ball fell, bouncing heavily on the filthy carpet before lying still.

I found the scrap of velvet and gently wrapped it around the ball, my fingers shaking as I tried to knot the ends together to form a bag.

That spell, or whatever I had just done, had taken everything out of me. I focused again and again, forcing my trembling fingers to fumble their way through the knots. Finally, it was done, and I fell to my knees in exhausted relief.

The sun was pouring in through the front window. The west-facing window. How many hours had passed? When had I lost track of time? In the other world? How long had Mina hovered over me, watching my last breaths?

I picked up the bundle of velvet and crystal and tried to get back to my feet, but it wasn't happening.

I wasn't afraid this time. It didn't feel like it was even really happening. I just accepted that walking was out of the question and started to crawl towards the front door. I had some vague idea if I could just get to that door, that everything would be okay.

Which was ridiculous. No one was there.

But there was. I heard a knock. I struggled with my too-thick tongue to answer, fumbled at crawling with a wand and a velvet-wrapped crystal ball in my hands. Then there was a second more insistent knock.

Mina had no family or friends. So who was at the door? Lawyers? Police following up on something?

My hand slipped out from under me, and I landed hard on my shoulder. I heard the thud but didn't feel myself hit the floor. My whole body was numb. I tried to call out but could only manage a slight burble of noise.

There was a ringing in my ears, ever louder, but I was sure that the third knock at the door was excessively violent. Then something was lifting me, shaking me. I couldn't seem to open my eyes, but the jostling shook them loose like a doll's eyes.

Someone's face was right in front of mine. Not Mina's.

"Edward?" I said or tried to.

But those weren't brown eyes. They were green. Dark green with little gold flecks, like sunlight through summer leaves.

I was shaking again, shivering and being shook both at once. I heard someone yelling. I caught the word "hospital."

"No," I said, clutching someone's sleeve and finally managing to drag myself back into the waking world. I dug my fingers in deep until Nick was looking at me. I only had the energy to form a single word. I had to make it count.

"School," I said.

Then I guess my eyes just rolled back because I knew no more.

CHAPTER 23

I slowly became aware that I was awake, but I was super reluctant to open my eyes. What if I had only pushed back the poison again? Was I still just moments away from dying?

I let my eyes stay closed as I focused on my breathing, then moved my awareness around my body. Just like Sophie had taught me. It had never put me in contact with my magic, but this was the second time I'd used it to just really assess how I was feeling.

I was feeling better, so much better. I was a little sore, but nothing like I expected. More like I'd been lying in this bed for days and days and needed to get up and move around a little. Only I also felt too weak to try that. I caught a bad flu once in junior high that kept me out of school for an entire week. I felt like I did then, the day after the fever finally broke.

But all sense of the poison in my body was gone. No headache, no numbness or muscle aches.

I thought I was going to be okay.

I opened my eyes to find warm sun spilling across my bed. My window faced east, so I guessed it was mid-morning, and the long spell of cold, gray weather had finally broken.

I tried sitting up, but that was too drastic a movement, and quickly settled for just hiking myself up a little higher on my pillow. I didn't realize until there was a long intake of breath that I wasn't alone, and my movement had woken someone sitting in the chair by the window, shaded by the tall winged chair back.

"Amanda?" It was Nick. He sounded like he was at some indefinite point between sleep and wakefulness.

"You brought me home," I said, pushing a matted mass of hair out of my eyes.

"Yeah," he said, still somewhat sleepy but coming out of it. He slid out of the chair to sit on the edge of my bed. "You told me to. Up until this minute, I was sure that had been a mistake. How are you feeling?"

"Better," I said. "Where are Brianna and Sophie?"

"Sleeping," he said. "It was a long night. I don't think they were sure they could save you. It took everything they had. I promised I would stay up with you so they could rest, but I guess it was a long night for me, too."

"Thank you," I said, reaching out to touch his hand. He took it and gave it a squeeze. With the sun behind him, it was hard to see his face, to read his expression.

"I'm glad you brought me home," I said. "I know you wanted to take me to a hospital, but I'm not sure they could've helped me."

"Yeah," he said. His hand around mine was so warm.

"Can I ask, why did you? Why did you listen to me?"

"Well," he said and gave a humorless laugh. "Well, I found you there on the floor. And there was what could only be a magic wand by your right hand, and this crystal ball half-rolled out of a velvet bag by your left hand. And it wasn't like any crystal ball I've ever seen at the Renaissance Festival or whatever. This was like real, dense glass with a dark heart."

"A very dark heart," I agreed. "You didn't touch it?"

"No," he said. "You don't touch the evidence at a crime scene."

"Crime scene?" I repeated, and this time I managed to sit up. "The police have it? And my wand?"

"No," Nick said. "Sit back, now. You're supposed to be resting."

"Where is it?" I said, not letting him push me back into the mound of pillows.

"Your wand is there," he said, pointing with his chin to the nightstand, where my wand sat on a square of linen edged with lace.

"And the crystal ball?"

"Brianna has it somewhere, I don't know," he said, but knowing Brianna had it was enough for me.

"Sorry, I didn't mean to alarm you," he said. "I should be more specific. I knew I was in a crime scene. That was obvious. But with the wand and the crystal ball and other little things I've been wondering about since I met you, I guess I figured there was more going on than I was supposed to understand. You asked me to bring you here. So I gathered up the wand and the ball and you and brought you all here."

"Thank you," I said.

"You came close to dying a couple of times," he said.

"I came close to dying a few times before you even got there," I said, closing my eyes in weariness at just the memory.

"Brianna didn't say so, but I could tell she thought I'd brought you here too late. But she never gave up, and neither did Sophie." The weariness was building, and I could feel myself drifting in and out, but I held on to the sound of his voice and to the feel of his hand on mine. "I might need you to explain some things to me. Later, when you're stronger."

"We're witches," I said, eyes still closed.

"That much I got," he said.

"Not so much me as Brianna and Sophie," I said. "They're the ones that have real power. Not me."

I started to doze a little but woke with a jolt, certain I was alone and feeling bereft. But Nick was still there.

"How did you find me?" I asked. "No one knew where I was going."

"You were gone a long time," he said. "Brianna and Sophie got worried. All they knew was that you told Brianna you were looking for me. So they found me, and the three of us figured out there were only a couple of places you could have gone. They sent me to Mina's house while they went to check some other places."

I touched the amulet under the cloth of my nightshirt, my 1927 Yankees jersey. I knew where they would have gone to check, where Nick couldn't go.

"Hey," I said, as more memories surfaced. "Did you break into Mina Fox's house without cause?"

Even with the sun behind him, I could see his cheeks flush.

"Obviously, I heard you call out," he said, clearing his throat nervously.

"I don't think so," I said. "I wanted to. I mean, I didn't know it was you, but someone was there. And I tried to yell, but I couldn't do it." Nick tried to pull away, but I caught his hand with both of mine. "You broke into an old woman's house without cause."

"I had cause," Nick said.

"Sure you did," I said, but teasing him was exhausting, so I let it go.

I was nearly off to sleep again when Nick called softly, "Amanda?"

"Hmm?" I said.

"Mina is gone. Isn't she?"

"Far, far away," I said.

"She killed Mrs. Olson. Didn't she?"

"Yes, she did," I said.

"Sophie found a hatpin in your yard, she said. She turned it over to the police yesterday before they even noticed you were missing."

"Hmm."

"It was the murder weapon?"

"Yes."

He was quiet then for a moment before asking, "Justice was done?"

I opened my eyes and tried to look into his, but that sun was just too bright. "Justice was done. I'm not an eye for an eye kind of person. I didn't execute her or anything. But Mina Fox will never hurt anyone again."

"Okay," he said, but he didn't sound quite satisfied with my answer. I had a feeling he had just filed that under the heading of things he'd ask me more about later when I was back on my feet.

"What happens with the house and the will and everything?" I asked.

"I don't know," he said. "She hadn't technically inherited anything yet. The will was in review. But she, like Linda Olson, had no next of kin. I think the state will probably get it."

"Good," I said. My eyes were still closed, and he probably thought I had gone back to sleep, but my mind was racing.

The thing in the crystal ball and Mina had been conspiring to get that house. I was sure because it was next to the school. The time portal. It was possible there would be others who wanted to be close to us, maybe allies, but more likely foes. Sophie, Brianna and I would have to be on our guard.

Always on our guard, never resting. And I was going to have to start being a little smarter. I couldn't let them down again.

CHAPTER 24

The next time I woke up, I was alone and definitely ready to get out of bed. I untangled myself from blankets and bedsheets and made my way to the window.

The sun was rising over the ridge on the opposite side of the river I couldn't quite see through all the trees. So I had slept all day and all night. No wonder my muscles were so achy and desperate to move around.

I dressed, pulled my tangles of hair back into a scrunchie, and jammed my bare feet into my sneakers, then made my way down the back stairs and out into the yard.

I don't think I was necessarily expecting to see anyone or do anything in particular, but when I slipped out the back door and saw Sophie and Brianna sitting on mats in the center of the orchard with another spare mat forming a circle with theirs, I wasn't surprised. I sat down on the extra mat and closed my eyes, joining them in silent meditation until I felt the sun shining over our back wall.

All three of us opened our eyes at once.

"How's the portal?" I asked.

"Still can't sense it?" Sophie asked.

"I think I could, but it's overwhelming," I said. "I can't see it from here; I have to go to this other place."

"Interesting," Brianna said and took out her notebook to scribble some notes.

"It's looking good now," Sophie said, her fingertips lightly resting on her crossed ankles as she gazed up into the middle distance between her and the sky.

"Now? Not before?" I asked.

"Things were weird when you were gone," Sophie said. "I was dealing with that. That's why I didn't notice you weren't here."

"I was in the library," Brianna said with heartbreaking glumness.

"Guys, I'm not blaming you for a thing," I said. "I had to go, and I had to go alone. It was that compulsion thing. It had to be that way."

"Hmm," Sophie said with the air of someone who was definitely prepared to argue the point at a later date.

"So when I was gone," I said, looking up at the sky. "Something was missing here, right?"

"Missing," Sophie said. "I don't know if I'd describe it that way. Nothing came through from 1927, that's for sure. But the portal itself was... not right."

"It almost collapsed," I guessed.

"But Miss Zenobia said that couldn't happen," Brianna said, but Sophie just frowned as she compared my words to her experience.

"She said she couldn't do it," I said. "She didn't say whether that was a lack of power or of will."

"Of will?" Brianna asked, her forehead wrinkling.

"I met her sister," I said. "Juno, her name is. She's been removed from the flow of time."

"What?" Sophie asked.

"She's the one who gave me the power when Helen attacked me," I said. "I thought at the time it was something in the house, but it wasn't."

"She moved you across time when we didn't," Brianna said.

"I think so," I said. "And somehow she helped Cora get the hatpin across to Mina. I think sending just that object through and back again, it would be too small for your devices to detect."

"Maybe," Brianna said. "I'll run some tests."

"You saw this Juno again the day before yesterday?" Sophie asked.

"Yes. She offered to save me again," I said. "I turned her down."

"You saved yourself," Sophie said with a twist of a smile.

"I think that was a team effort, don't you?" I said, looking from her to Brianna. They both avoided meeting my eyes. I knew Nick was right; they had nearly lost me several times. But they hadn't.

"So this thing with Cora and Mina and the hatpin and everything, she made that happen?" Sophie asked.

"I don't think so. I mean, I think she helped sneak the murder weapon around, but Mina and Cora were both taking orders from the crystal ball."

"That thing," Brianna said, wrinkling her nose up in disgust.

"Juno said that it was outside of time," I said. "It only exists for a fixed set of points, but the thing inside it experiences every moment of time simultaneously."

"The thing?" Brianna repeated. "Amanda, you know what it is."

"I don't," I said.

"But you put her there," Brianna said.

"No," I said. "I put Mina inside of it. I thought it was just to imprison her there with that thing she was conspiring with for all time. But I don't know a thing about what was in there in the first place."

"It was Mina," Brianna said. "It was always Mina."

"A Mina demented by..." Sophie broke off, scratching her head. "I was going to say demented by ages trapped in that sphere, but if what you said is true, would she have any perception of time at all?"

"No perception of time passing doesn't mean that it would seem short," Brianna said. "It could seem like she just got there, that she's always been there, and every state in between. All at once, every moment."

"No sense of progression of time," I said. "No story."

"Damn, that's cold," Sophie said.

"I didn't do it on purpose," I said. "I was trying to be humane. I was about to collapse from the poison again, and after I recovered the first time, she would surely find a way to finish the job the second time. I had to do something. I didn't want to kill her."

"So what do we do with it now?" Sophie asked. "Surely we can't destroy it. Can we get her back out?"

"I don't think that would be wise," Brianna said. "I have it sealed in one of Miss Zenobia's safe boxes. It's warded and protected."

"But she's still inside it," I said.

"I know," Brianna said sadly. "I'll do more research. There's probably a way to fix the time thing. To make her more quiescent. To at least stop the torment."

"It's my mistake," I said. "I should fix it."

"We're a team," Sophie said. "We play to each other's strengths. Let Bree do the research thing."

"And Sophie can monitor the portal for changes," Brianna said. "In case the other day is just the start of some new sort of pattern."

"You say Juno came through the portal and disrupted things when she came to talk to you?" Sophie asked.

"No, that's not it," I said. "Juno *is* the time portal."

The two of them just stared at me, dumbfounded.

"She told you that?" Sophie asked at last.

"Not exactly, but I'm sure that's what's going on," I said.

"But you said she was Miss Zenobia's sister," Brianna said.

"Juno has been removed from time," I said. "She doesn't interact with anything here. She can only see me when I'm in my altered state where I see all the silvery lines and webs and things, and she's not connected to anything when she's there. She's just… free-floating."

"But such a thing would take enormous amounts of magic," Brianna said, then shook her head. "I don't think it's even possible."

"But if it were," Sophie said slowly, "Miss Zenobia would have been the witch able to do it."

"And if she had," I went on, "she must have had a good reason. It saddened her, I could tell on that night she spoke to us. She had regret about her sister."

Sophie scrunched up her face, trying to remember the words I recalled.

"And that's why she stayed here until she died?" Brianna asked. "She was already an old witch when she came here. That's unusual. Most witches find their haunts when they're young and hunker down to watch the centuries roll by."

"Not always," Sophie said. "There are nomads as well."

"Exceptions," Brianna said. "Miss Zenobia wasn't one of them."

"We need to understand this better," I said. "We swore an oath to protect this place, but we weren't given all the facts."

We lapsed into separate thoughts again. I was starting to feel a bit cold sitting outside in October on a thin yoga mat. I got up and stretched my back, and a sudden pang of hunger struck me. "I'm going to get some breakfast," I said.

"Good idea," Sophie said, rising up to her feet like some giant had pulled up on an invisible thread on the top of her head.

"Wait," Brianna said, not looking up at us as she scribbled more notes in her book. We waited. "What about Cora?" she asked as she put the book away.

"What about her?" I asked as we walked together back to the porch.

"We can't just let her get away with it," Brianna said.

"As far as I can tell, all she did was take her daughter's hatpin, then return it later," I said. "I'm not convinced she even knew why. She was just doing what that crystal ball told her to do."

"That ball had power in the past," Sophie said. "But when Brianna and I looked at it here, nothing."

"That is weird," I said. Then Brianna exclaimed aloud, slapping her own forehead.

"What?" Sophie asked.

"It was never from the ball," Brianna said. "I ran so many tests, but I just wasn't thinking."

"What are you talking about, Bree?" Sophie asked again.

"Um, I tried to trigger the ball again," Brianna said. "Yesterday, while you both were sleeping. But it wouldn't do anything. I thought maybe it was just me; it didn't care about me. But it hated you,

Amanda. And yet it never attacked you at Mina's house, did it? That was all Mina."

"I thought Mina was the ball," Sophie said.

"Yes, but all she can do is whisper," Brianna said. "She creeped Cora out, and she bonded in a really creepy way with her own self, but what about Margery?"

"She scared Margery," I said.

"Margery, who knew her mother was a fraud, but who also knew in a deep down to the bone way that magic was nevertheless real."

"You mean all that back in the house was Margery?" I asked.

"Margery was terrified," Sophie said.

"Yes, she was," Brianna said. "She had no training. She didn't know what she was doing. I don't think she even knew she was doing it."

We all fell silent. Then we went into the house to the waiting pot of coffee.

"Do we need to do something about that?" I wondered.

"I don't think so," Brianna said. "Cora fears that ball. After what happened, she's going to find a better way to hide that thing, to keep it quiet and secure. I mean, we sort of know she did, don't we?"

"If anything had happened like what we saw another time, there'd be stories," I agreed.

"But what about Cora?" Sophie asked. "Do we just let that go? Maybe she didn't know what she was doing moving that hatpin around, but maybe she did. Maybe she knew she was an accomplice to murder, even framing her own daughter for it."

"Maybe she didn't," Brianna said.

"Why put the pin back, though?" I pondered. "Was the ball commanding Mina and Cora just to frame Margery?"

"No," Sophie said. "It knew we would find it. It was using the pin to lure us there."

"Why?" Brianna asked.

"Because the ball was just whispers, and Mina as a human had no power, but Margery did," I said.

"Mina and the ball couldn't destroy us, but Margery very nearly did," Sophie said. "But she didn't mean to. I definitely never sensed an ill intent."

"No, she can't control what she does," I agree. "And we know from what Mina told us about her childhood that Margery never used that power. I think the best thing we can do is not meddle and let Margery take care of herself."

"If only there *were* a witches' council," Brianna said glumly. "Advice would be so fantastic right now."

"But there's still the matter of Cora. Maybe she didn't mean to set her own daughter up to take the rap for a murder, or to bring us to her with the intent of her murdering us all. But what's not a maybe is that Cora was using people's personal information to rip them off," Sophie said. "Are we going to do anything about that?"

"It's really more of a legal matter than a witch one," Brianna said. "Maybe we should meddle."

"No, we should totally meddle," I said.

"Not confrontationally," Sophie quickly added, although if there was a girl always ready for a confrontation, it was Sophie. "In fact, I have the perfect idea."

CHAPTER 25

*J*was fussing with my dress again, I admit it, but Sophie
didn't have to slap my hand so hard.

"Hey," I said, cradling my stinging hand.

"Leave it alone," she said in a very motherly tone. "Honestly, you
look great."

"If you say so," I said, but I wasn't being entirely fair. Sophie had
planted me in front of a mirror after she had finished dressing me and
doing my hair, and even I had to admit I had never looked so good.
She had the same magic touch with my hair that she had with her own
little patch of curls that always perfectly framed her face.

Okay, maybe that wasn't strictly speaking magic. But it was
certainly a thing I knew I could never be taught. She had gotten my
cowlick to cooperate without even beating it into submission first,
sweeping my hair back and holding it in place with a band that had a
peacock feather that curled just so around my ear.

Clearly, if I didn't leave everything just the way she'd done it, I'd
ruin everything. I clasped my hands together and promised I'd be
good.

"So, this is the last of them?" Brianna asked as she peered into milk
crates filled with packages all wrapped, sealed, and addressed.

"It's the last of them," Sophie said. "That's why we're celebrating. It's taken days for Margery and me to compile this all together."

"And a small fortune in gin to keep Cora out of Margery's hair," Otto said as he came into the room. We were in his lair under the former beer hall. I didn't know what he and Sophie had planned for our little impromptu celebration, but I really hoped it wasn't going to be happening upstairs. That seemed like a rough crowd in the middle of the day; I'd hate to see what they got up to after dark.

"And the crystal ball stopped whispering to her?" I asked after Otto had picked up an armful of packages and gone back out of the cellar.

"Yes," Sophie said.

"I told you when I put it in the safe box under ward, it lost its power in every point of time," Brianna said.

I held up a hand. "Please don't try to explain that to me again. I just get confused."

"You only have to remember that since we did the spell, we're considered the prime timeline—" Brianna started to say, but gave up as both Sophie and I roared our protests over her.

"Please," I said, laughing. "It's not going to make more sense on the hundredth try. Margery is safe; that's all I need to know."

"And you look good," Sophie said. "Tell her that too."

"You look great, Brianna," I said, and she flushed in maximum introvert discomfort. Sophie had insisted on dressing her up too, in a shade of emerald green that made her hair look like the brightest red-gold imaginable. And she did a much better job than I did with not fussing with the frippery.

"Last batch?" Edward as he walked up to the table and picked up the last of the milk crates.

"Last batch," Sophie confirmed after a quick look around.

"Great. Otto is going to have Benny bring the car around, but he's got something to get the party started here first." Then he winked at me and headed back up the stairs.

"He likes you," Brianna said in her usual just stating facts voice.

"Nonsense," I said. "He's looking to marry Coco's sister Ivy."

"He's looking to marry *up*," Sophie said wryly. "He's not given it anything like the correct amount of thought, including the fact that's he's already on his way up on his own if he'd just look around and appreciate it. Plus. You are most definitely up. And he does like you."

"I think the ninety years between us are going to be a problem," I said, then looked around for anything at all to change the subject. "Is this really going to work?"

"My master plan?" Sophie asked. "You're questioning my master plan?"

"Well," I said.

"It won't work with everyone," Brianna said. "Even with every scrap of evidence returned to them, every purloined and copied letter, every overheard scrap of gossip reported to them, some still won't believe that Cora really intended ill."

"Being a medium is terribly hard work, you know," Sophie said sarcastically. "Sometimes the spirits need assistance. Hints. Just to get them started. It doesn't mean that it isn't all true."

"Some will never change their minds," Brianna said. "But enough will. Maybe enough for her to have to pack up and head further west. Poor Margery."

"Not just Margery," I said. "I see a lot of household servants about to get sacked."

"It's a dying profession anyway," Sophie said, but I could tell that was the only part of the plan that wasn't sitting entirely comfortably with her. Just as I had, she found a way to change the subject. "What are we going to do about Miss Zenobia and her sister?"

"I've searched and searched, but if Miss Zenobia kept anything like a diary, there's no sign of it," Brianna said.

"It would be nice to talk to her again," I said.

"Not possible," Brianna said.

"I know, you said," I sighed. "It would just make everything so much easier if we could just ask."

"Who's to say if we could that she wouldn't just lie?" Sophie asked. "She wasn't entirely truthful before, it seems."

"Maybe I can find things written about her by other people. Get a picture of things that way," Brianna said.

"We can always talk to Juno, for what that's worth," I said. "Although I think she lied more than Miss Zenobia did."

"Without any sense of what's true, we have no way of knowing," Sophie said.

"Are we pawns? Like Cora said?" Brianna asked.

Sophie groaned aloud. "Cora was messing with us to put us off our game and elevate her own position. Nothing she said meant anything."

But I shared Brianna's worry. If we were pawns in a battle that Miss Zenobia had started with her sister, and she had left us behind to keep her sister bound for all time… what was the correct thing to do?

"I don't know if we can tell who's right and who's wrong between the two of them," I said. "I suspect there was right and wrong on both sides."

"Probably not in equal measure," Sophie pointed out.

"No, likely not," I agreed. "Still, I think we can agree on one thing."

"What's that?" Brianna asked.

"If we can't rely on the generation who came before us, we can only rely on ourselves. Ourselves, and each other," I said.

"I'll drink to that," Sophie said, looking around for something to drink.

As if summoned by her words, Edward and Otto came through the doorway together, Otto with a bottle of champagne in a bucket of ice in his arms and Edward with fluted glasses laced between his fingers.

"You know, I really should move to some nicer digs, don't you think?" Otto said, looking up at the cobwebs hanging from the beer-stained rafters.

"Something above ground, maybe?" Sophie suggested.

"Now, let's not get crazy here," Otto said, pulling the champagne out of the bucket and popping the cork.

"Just a little taste to get the evening started," Otto said as he filled the glasses. "Then we're crossing the river. There's a terrific new band playing at the Wabasha Street Speakeasy. You're going to love it."

I took a sip of champagne, which promptly went straight up my nose. But I didn't even mind. I was wearing a gorgeous dress, my hair looked good just for once, and I was going out to hear real Jazz Age jazz with a—let's face it—bootlegging gangster and a cute boy who wasn't looking for anything serious from me. It was the recipe for just one perfect night. That's all that I needed.

The epic battles of not-quite-good versus maybe-not-so-evil could wait until another day.

CHECK OUT BOOK THREE!

The Witches Three will return in Third Time is a Charm, out now!

Amanda Clarke possesses the rarest, most powerful form of magic: the ability to see and manipulate time itself.

If only she knew how to use it. All she gets are vague impressions, little intuitions that compel her to act.

When she pays a visit to her friend Nick's apartment, one of her witchy feelings is warning her about the apartment across the hall. The empty apartment. The apartment no one has gone in or out of in years.

She promises Nick to follow the rules this time. But the feeling won't be ignored. She gathers the Witches Three and they magic their way inside.

And find a body dressed for 1927 but still warm and only recently dead in 2018. Yet another case beyond the local police department, but perfect for the Witches Three.

Third Time is a Charm, Book 3 in the Witches Three Cozy Mystery Series!

THE VIKING WITCH COZY MYSTERIES

In case you missed it, check out Body at the Crossroads, the first book in the Viking Witch Cozy Mystery Series!

When her mother dies after a long illness, Ingrid Torfa must sell the family home to cover the medical bills. Her career as a book illustrator not yet exactly launched, Ingrid faces two options: live in her battered old Volkswagen, or go back to her mother's small town in northern Minnesota.

The small town that still haunts her dreams more than a decade since she last visited it. Or rather, not the town but the grandmother.

All of the drawings she fills notebooks with witches and the trolls that do their bidding? Not as whimsical in her nightmares as she sketches them in the bright light of day.

If not for her beloved cat Mjolner, living in the Volkswagen just might tempt her.

But the cat wants four walls and a door, so north she goes. And finds trouble in the form of a dead body before she even finds her grandmother's little town. How much can a town of stoic fishermen possibly be hiding?

As Ingrid is about to find out, quite a lot.

Body at the Crossroads, the first book in the Viking Witch Cozy Mystery Series!

THE WEAL & WOE BOOKSHOP
WITCH MYSTERIES

In case you missed it, check out The Teashop Terror, the first book in the new Weal & Woe Bookshop Witch Mystery Series!

No one knows more about every branch of magic than Tabitha Greene. She devoted years to studying the most esoteric texts, hunting down the most obscure source materials, and deciphering the most cryptic ancient scrolls. But her career in academia hits a dead end when no wizard will take her on as an apprentice.

Just because, despite being descended from two long and prestigious lines of witches, her attempts to actually perform any magic always fail. Often spectacularly.

But no more college means no more dorm life. And no magical skills means no real job skills, at least, not in the witchy world. And a life spent moving from school to school every few months was a life without real friendships. She finds herself alone with nowhere to go.

Then an uncle she barely remembers offers her a summer job, running his bookstore over the summer. The Weal and Woe Bookstore, located in a magical pocket world within a block of buildings just north of the old Mill District of Minneapolis, Minnesota.

Not exactly the pinnacle of all her hopes and dreams. But it's just for one summer, right?

Or so Tabitha tells herself. But unbeknownst to her, the Weal and Woe Bookstore is about to change her life.

The Teashop Terror, the first book in the new Weal & Woe Bookshop Witch Mystery Series!

ALSO FROM RATATOSKR PRESS

The Ritchie and Fitz Sci-Fi Murder Mysteries starts with Murder on the Intergalactic Railway.

For Murdina Ritchie, acceptance at the Oymyakon Foreign Service Academy means one last chance at her dream of becoming a diplomat for the Union of Free Worlds. For Shackleton Fitz IV, it represents his last chance not to fail out of military service entirely.

Strange that fate should throw them together now, among the last group of students admitted after the start of the semester. They had once shared the strongest of friendships. But that all ended a long time ago.

But when an insufferable but politically important woman turns up murdered, the two agree to put their differences aside and work together to solve the case.

Because the murderer might strike again. But more importantly, solving a murder would just have to impress the dour colonel who clearly thinks neither of them belong at his academy.

Murder on the Intergalactic Railway, the first book in the Ritchie and Fitz Sci-Fi Murder Mysteries, available everywhere books are sold.

FREE EBOOK!

Like exclusive, free content?

If you'd like to receive "A Collection of Witchy Prequels", a free collection of short story prequels to the Witches Three Cozy Mystery and Viking Witch Cozy Mystery series, as well as other free stories throughout the year, go to my website CateMartin.com to subscribe to my newsletter! This eBook is exclusively for newsletter subscribers and will never be sold in stores. Check it out!

ABOUT THE AUTHOR

Cate Martin has written stories which have appeared in *Mystery, Crime and Mayhem* quarterly magazine as well as in the annual *Holiday Spectacular* Advent calendar of Christmas stories. She is also the author of three witch mystery series: *The Witches Three Cozy Mysteries*, and *The Viking Witch Cozy Mysteries* and *The Weal and Woe Bookshop Witch Mysteries*. She currently lives in Minneapolis, Minnesota. You can learn more about her work at CateMartin.com.

ALSO BY CATE MARTIN

The Witches Three Cozy Mystery Series

Charm School

Work Like a Charm

Third Time is a Charm

Old World Charm

Charm his Pants Off

Charm Offensive

The Witches Three Cozy Mysteries Books 1-3

The Witches Three Cozy Mysteries Books 4-6

The Viking Witch Cozy Mystery Series

Body at the Crossroads

Death Under the Bridge

Murder on the Lake

Killing in the Village Commons

Bloodshed in the Forest

Corpse in the Mead Hall

Slaying on the Lake Shore

Bones by the Forest Road

Sacrifice Behind the Falls

Body Under the Café

Assassination in the Glade

Bewitchment After the Storm (available July 9, 2024 direct from me or August 13, 2024 in stores everywhere)

The Viking Witch Cozy Mysteries Books 1-3

The Viking Witch Cozy Mysteries Books 4-6

The Weal & Woe Bookshop Witch Mystery Series

The Teashop Terror

The Salon & Spa Scandal

The Bookseller Blunder

The Entrepreneur Enigma

The Novelty Shop Nightmare (available August 13, 2024 direct from me or September 10, 2024 in stores everywhere)

The Courtyard Conundrum (available December 10, 2024 direct from me or January 14, 2025 in stores everywhere)